# Golpes bajos / Low Blows

Para Almaida y Karisa
con mis mejores deseos
Alri, 2007

THE AMERICAS

*Series Editors:*

ILAN STAVANS and IRENE VILAR

■

*Advisory Board:*

Homero Aridjis

Ariel Dorfman

Rosario Ferré

Jean Franco

Alvaro Mutis

Mirta Ojito

Margaret Sayers Peden

Luis J. Rodriguez

Bob Shacochis

Antonio Skármeta

Doug Unger

The University of Wisconsin Press

# Golpes bajos / Low Blows

## Instantáneas / Snapshots

# Alicia Borinsky

Translated by
Cola Franzen and the author

Foreword by
Michael Wood

The University of Wisconsin Press

The University of Wisconsin Press
1930 Monroe Street
Madison, Wisconsin 53711

www.wisc.edu/wisconsinpress/

3 Henrietta Street
London WC2E 8LU, England

1    3    5    4    2

Printed in the United States of America

Library of Congress Cataloging-in-Publication Data
Borinsky, Alicia.
Golpes bajos: instantáneas = Low blows: snapshots / Alicia Borinsky;
translated by Cola Franzen and the author; foreword by Michael Wood.
      p.      cm. — (The Americas)
ISBN 0-299-21600-4 (cloth: alk. paper)
1. Borinsky, Alicia — Translations into English.
2. Buenos Aires (Argentina) — Social life and customs — Fiction.
I. Franzen, Cola.   II. Title.   III. Title: Low Blows.
PQ7798.12.O687A2       2007
863′.64 — dc22        2006031484

for
JEFFREY,
who knows

# Contents

## La mujer invisible / The Invisible Woman

## Rincón de los profetas / Prophet's Corner

¡Sonreí! Te estamos autobiografiando /
Smile! We Are Autobiographing You

## Locas / Fruitcakes

# Foreword

*Anyone see where the joke came from?*

The world of *Golpes bajos / Low Blows* is not hard to find, since it is the world we know, the one we see all around us, in the streets, cafes, houses, apartments, prisons, and dance halls of wherever we are. But would we have seen it, would we recognize the familiarity in its strangeness, without Alicia Borinsky's help? Surely not. These pieces of limpid, quirky, simple, and fantastic prose offer us pictures of recognizable human occasions, but they are "snapshots," as the subtitle of the book suggests, only in a special sense. They don't photograph ready-made scenes; they compose scenes in the camera of language, and what comes out is not a copy of the real but a reordering of it. The metaphor of photography is very appropriate, though. The prose catches the equivalent of passing moments; nearly ninety instances of life become briefly, comically, desperately visible before they lapse back into ordinary invisibility. The title of one of the book's sections tells an intricate little story: "Smile! We Are Autobiographing You." That is, we are taking not just a picture of your life, but also a picture of your picture of your life.

Certain phrases recur, giving us a clue for our navigation between geography and fantasy. "In this country," "in that country," "in that city"; "once there was," "in another time there was"; and even, bringing these two kinds of beginning together, "Once there was a country." The city is Buenos Aires, it seems, and also a fairy-tale forest; the country is Argentina, and also any place on earth where politics, however violent or terminal, seems a dream or a fable. "Once there was a country," the narrator tells us, "with so many doctors that the military junta . . . organized a civil war so the doctors would have plenty of work." However, the long spell of unemployment before the war (the doctors' only skill was getting paid illegally by chemical and pharmaceutical companies) means they don't know how to attend the dead and wounded, and the country demands action. The doctors are all killed, and as the piece ends the country is still celebrating, even five years after the event. Here we have a political fable,

an international joke about doctors, a Latin American joke about military juntas (not above "organizing" civil wars for their own purposes), and a more general discreet reminder of the incidental suffering and dying that goes on in any country that hasn't managed to escape from history.

We are in the same real and imaginary realm when we read the prose portrait of a model citizen. He "has never participated in any demonstrations or attended the official ceremonies in which we decorate those who have never criticized us." He is not interested in sports or money, and therefore—the surprise of the logic is truly chilling—he will make an ideal candidate for torture and will confess his secret as soon as electric shocks are applied to his body. What secret? Will it have a political meaning? Will the torture have a purpose? No. The purpose of torture is torture, and we realize as we reach the end of the paragraph that Borinsky's speaker is himself one of the torturers. The unfortunate man will tell "us" his secret, and the torturer delights in the very idea of the efficacy of the shocks. What has happened here is that a historical reality has been drained of its supposed practical meaning, leaving only its concrete but disconnected result: the gratuitous pain of one person and the ugly pleasure of another.

But not all is political in this wonderful book. There are marriages falling apart and (barely) hanging together; there are many lonely people who have harebrained schemes for getting themselves some company; there are many "invisible" women, as the title of one section reminds us. There are even invisible children who turn into invisible women. One of them is the result of a "birth almost without a moan" that is entirely without celebration. No one remembers her name, and our narrator, mingling self-accusation with compassion, says, "Personally I confess to you that I do not envy her and for me, as you know, that is very special, that's saying a lot."

The many children in the volume give a perfect measure of its tone, its brilliant ironies and its secret sympathies. There is the little girl who is born of a scandal ("Nací de chiquita," she says, "I was born when I was a little girl") but finds a form of freedom in the sheer malice of her grown-up relatives: they are too mean to be worth obeying or helping. There is the couple who decide to have orphans as children—not to adopt children but to beget children who will feel like orphans—because they are drawn to the silent, formal behavior

of infants raised in institutions. And there is the children's choir, about to sing, as the prose piece ends, the nightmare the music teacher told her favorite pupil about yesterday. Singing, silent, rebelling, these children are snapshots of snapshots, versions of what we forget, and what this book so infallibly remembers.

At times the book turns to pure epigram: "Prophets are never wrong when they are lying"; "Of all her loves his was the only one that left her whole"; "I've been very happy in his arms, above all when I thought of all the movies we would watch together." Like all good epigrams, these instances tell us the truth and make us laugh—and mock the wordiness of most of the rest of our lives. And then there are Borinsky's witty, endlessly irreverent titles. They multiply the meanings of all the pieces, and sometimes invert them, as in a curved mirror. The title of the epigram about the prophets, for example, is "house gift for newlyweds"; the one about several loves is called "From the Heart," literally "I keep you in my soul," as if life were just a bolero gone wrong. Perhaps the funniest and most haunting title is the one that precedes a desperate letter ("Dearest treasure: I felt so lost when you up and left me"): "Anyone See Where the Shot Came From?"

*Golpes bajos / Low Blows* is a book of surprises, full of turns of language and imagination that constantly catch us off guard. This is why it is so strange that we should finally know where we are, and why we are lucky to make it back to the once-familiar world. We are so used to solemn failures of sight that we scarcely know what to do with lightness of glance and many-angled vision.

MICHAEL WOOD

# Preface

I have worked with Cola Franzen to reproduce in English the irony, black humor, and rhythm of the original Spanish. Ours is a literary translation. We have not left aside literal solutions altogether but we have chosen, instead, to focus on creating English versions faithful to the cultural differences between the two languages. We strived for a language as easy and flowing as the Spanish original.

A great part of the pleasure of bilingual editions consists in the counterpoint created by the presentation of texts that speak to what lies in between languages, the thrill of finding how the same effects may be created in a language with very different cultural associations from the original. It is in this sense that we have remained close to the original even if it meant departing from the most obvious and literal translation.

We hope that readers knowing both languages will enjoy savoring this game of hide-and-seek in the present volume and that those who read it in one language will learn something about the other.

ALICIA BORINSKY

# Acknowledgments

The author and the translator would like to thank Wolfgang Franzen and Ezra B. Mehlman for their help and support in putting together this book.

# Entre nosotros /
# Between You and Me

# Buenos alumnos

Han llegado como si los hubieran convocado especialmente. Bien vestidos. Han dejado de ser niños y ahora se miran, controlan sus pasos en el pasillo porque pronto también ellos habrán de marchar. Al unísono y como quien no quiere la cosa se internarán en el salón de actos. En ese momento ella se estará riendo con el profesor de piano pero le bastará un instante para darse cuenta de que esta clase no será como las demás. Tensa, mirada a punto de cuajarse de lágrimas, dirigirá el coro que, disciplinado, cantará estentóreamente una pesadilla que le contó a su alumno preferido hace exactamente un día y quince minutos.

# Well-behaved Students

They've come in as if in answer to a special summons. Neatly dressed. Now no longer children, they look at each other, walk carefully through the corridor because soon they too will have to march. All together they will gingerly make their way into the auditorium. At that moment she will be laughing with the piano teacher but it'll take her only a second to realize that this class won't be like the others. Tense, on the verge of tears, she will direct the chorus that, well-trained, will sing in thunderous voice a nightmare she'd told her favorite student exactly a day plus fifteen minutes ago.

# Canto amoroso

## Historia en tres partes
### Primera y segunda para que entiendan el desenlace

En la primera parte deja al marido por un hombre de estatura mediana, pancita y ciento cinco mil dólares con veinte centavos en una cuenta bancaria en Suiza. Ella se llama Eugenia Francisca Carpani y a él sólo le gusta que lo llamen por su sobrenombre de Francisco Benedicto. Aunque Eugenia es diez años menor que él, Francisco Benedicto le pide consejo para todo, hasta para sus menesteres más mínimos incluyendo ciertas recetas para medialunas destinadas a la panadería que le legó su padre y en la cual ahora trabajan juntos. Eugenia extraña de vez en cuando a su marido debido a que la panadería se viene abajo derrotada por la competencia de las grandes cadenas que venden pan hecho por gente que habla idiomas de países donde ni siquiera se come pan pero cuyos salarios permiten la venta de su trabajo por sumas irrisorias en edificios iluminados por luces fluorescentes. Ninguno de los dos sabe de la cuenta en Suiza. Es regalo discreto de un tío tímido devorado por la culpa causada por una afrenta que ha dejado rastros incontrovertibles en el estilo con el cual Francisco Benedicto hace el amor todos los viernes de años impares. Como la historia de los amores de Eugenia y Francisco Benedicto es muy breve ella no se dará cuenta de que le debe sus placeres eróticos al tío.

La segunda parte de la historia empieza con una carta del joven y atlético marido de Eugenia, el abogado de la Cuesta, quien, incapaz de entender las razones del abandono, decide intervenir inmediatamente para que la municipalidad cierre la panadería y los deje a ambos de patitas en la calle. Cosa que, gracias a la sabia donación de una suma para la campaña de re-elección del alcalde, se logra de la noche a la mañana.

Querida Eugenia:

Me he enterado de la aciaga situación en que se encuentran tanto vos como tu amante. Es una pena que les hayan clausurado la única

4

# Love Song

Story in three parts
First and second so you'll understand the outcome

In the first part she leaves her husband for a man of medium height, little pot belly, and a hundred and five thousand dollars and twenty cents in a Swiss bank account. Her name is Eugenia Francisca Carpani and he likes to be called only by his given names Francisco Benedicto. Although Eugenia is ten years younger than he is, Francisco Benedicto asks her advice about everything, including even the smallest details such as certain recipes for croissants meant for the bakery left to him by his father and where the couple now work together. Once in a while Eugenia misses her husband because the bakery is going under, bankrupted by the competition of the big chains where they sell bread made by people who speak languages of countries where they don't even eat bread but whose salaries allow their work to be sold for outrageously low prices in buildings lit by fluorescent lights. Neither one of them knows about the Swiss account. It is a discreet gift from a shy uncle eaten up by guilt because of an insult that left indisputable marks on the way Francisco Benedicto makes love every Friday of odd-numbered years. Since the love story of Eugenia and Francisco Benedicto is very short, she will not realize that she owes her erotic pleasures to the uncle.

The second part of the story begins with a letter from Eugenia's young athletic husband, Tomás de la Cuesta, the lawyer, who, unable to understand the reasons why she abandoned him, decided to act immediately so that the city would close down the bakery and leave them high and dry on the street. Something that, thanks to the wise donation of a hefty contribution to the mayor's re-election campaign, happened overnight.

Dear Eugenia:
I have learned of the dire circumstances in which you and your lover find yourselves. It is a pity that the only source of income you

5

fuente de ingresos que les quedaba. Me imagino, sin embargo, que andarán buscando trabajo. No dejes de pensar en mí si necesitan alguna carta de recomendación. Quedo a tu disposición. Conoces mis horarios. Te pido encarecidamente que no me llames por teléfono a casa ya que mi actual mujer no comprendería la situación y le darían celos. Algún día te la presentaré para que ella, al verte, sepa que no debe temer nada. Hasta muy pronto, un saludo afectuoso de

Tomás
(firma con letra decidida y arrogante)

¿Qué habrá querido decir con eso de que comprendería que no tiene nada que temer? ¿Bastaba con verla? Naturalmente este es el momento del gran cambio cosmético. Partió raudamente a una peluquería, se compró maquillaje barato ya que no le alcanzaba para más y con eso, una pollera ajustada y tacos quedó exactamente como lo había previsto Tomás. Tenía la pinta exacta de una sirvienta endomingada. Así se fueron a verlo ella y su amante y así consiguieron el puesto de caseros con cama adentro. Quedaron agradecidísimos. Vivieron contemplando la felicidad adquisitiva de Tomás y su mujer que, extenuados de tanto exhibicionismo y shopping, un día se pelearon para siempre aunque siguieron viviendo juntos ya que no se dieron cuenta por falta de energía para buscar domicilios independientes, separar objetos que ya no les importaban y turnarse para cuidar las innumerables mascotas contrabandeadas por muchachos barbudos que los miraban con esa sonrisa rutilante dada por hongos exóticos y hierbas aromáticas.

Eugenia y Francisco Benedicto se quedaron en la cocina jugando a la canasta olvidados del romance que los había juntado. Cada uno había logrado silenciar la pasión del otro. Estaban tranquilos. Como todos los humillados. Juntaban presión sin estrategia, sin plan para cambiar sus circunstancias. Francisco Benedicto se distraía cuidando canarios y un día le dió el consabido contagio y se murió después de haberle atendido el granito de pus a un canario albino y secarse la uña con los labios. Por tratarse de un hombre sin medios simplemente tiraron su cadáver al río desde donde fue arrastrado por la corriente a la misma fosa de los ahogados en que estaba su tío, el millonario suicida. Entretanto, el hábil abogado utilizando sus relaciones en el mundo de la finanzas, obtuvo la llave de la caja donde estaba el

had has been closed. I imagine, though, that you will be looking for work. Remember me if you should need a letter of recommendation. I am at your service. You know my schedule. I do beg you urgently not to call me at home since my present wife would not understand the situation and would be jealous. Some day I will introduce you to her so that seeing you, she will know she has nothing to fear. Until very soon, with affectionate greetings from

Tomás
(signature written with strong, arrogant script)

What could he have meant by saying his wife would understand she had nothing to fear? It would be enough just to see her? Naturally it's time for a great cosmetic change. She left in a great hurry for a beauty salon, bought some cheap make-up since she could no longer afford the more expensive kind, and with it and a tight sweater and heels, she ended up exactly the way Tomás had foreseen—looking exactly like a maid in her Sunday outfit. She and her lover went to see Tomás and ended up getting the job of live-in housekeepers. They were enormously grateful. They lived contemplating the acquisitive happiness of Tomás and his wife who, exhausted from so much shopping and showing off, had their final fight one day although they continued to live together unaware they lacked energy to look for separate places, or to divide up objects they no longer cared about, or to take turns tending the countless mascots smuggled in by bearded guys who looked at them with that sparkling smile caused by exotic mushrooms and aromatic herbs.

Eugenia and Francisco Benedicto stayed in the kitchen playing canasta, the romance that had brought them together forgotten. Each one had managed to quiet the passion of the other. They were serene. Like all humiliated couples. They joined coercion with no strategy, no plan to change their circumstances. Francisco Benedicto amused himself by taking care of canaries and one day he caught the well-known disease and died after treating an albino canary's infected pimple and cleaning the claw with his lips. Since he was poor they simply tossed the cadaver into the river, where it was carried by the current to the same common grave of drowned people and where his uncle, the millionaire suicide, ended up. Meanwhile, Tomás, the clever lawyer, used his connections in financial circles to get

legado del tío y en un último esfuerzo por darle sentido y circulari-dad a su vida, la invitó a Eugenia a visitar Europa, cenar en Ginebra y culminar la velada con una apertura de la caja arreglada por el ge-rente del banco, un vendedor de armas que así aseguraba su discre-ción. Probablemente haya sido demasiado tarde para Eugenia que en este momento termina de romper el último billete en pedacitos muy pequeños. Su ex la mira perplejo, no porque esté preocupado por la pérdida de la fortuna sino porque no entiende cómo, habiéndose tragado tanto papel, no vomita o eructa o canta una de esas can-ciones que le escuchaba cuando estaba en la cocina.

possession of the key to the safety deposit box where the uncle's will was kept and in a final effort to give his life sense and circularity, he invited Eugenia to visit Europe with him, dine in Geneva, and end the evening by opening the box, arranged by the bank director, an arms dealer whose discretion could therefore be counted on. Probably it was too late for Eugenia who at this moment is tearing the last bill into very tiny pieces. Her ex looks at her perplexed, not because he cares about the loss of the fortune but because he cannot understand how after swallowing so much paper she neither vomits nor belches nor sings one of those songs he used to listen to when she was in the kitchen.

# Desencuentro

En esa casa una mujer llora frente a la ventana y el hombre que ha permanecido callado durante tres meses, cuatro días y cinco minutos, canta un aria que ella no entiende porque, a pesar de que ha perfeccionado hasta la decadencia su italiano, a él sólo le interesa cantar en alemán.

# Mismatch

In that house a woman is standing before the window weeping while the man who'd been silent for three months, four days, and five minutes sings an aria that she can't understand; although she's perfected her Italian to the $n$th degree, he only likes to sing in German.

# El concurso

Estimada Srta. Caruso:

Reciba nuestras calurosas felicitaciones por haber sido ganadora del concurso "31 de diciembre de 1999." Este año, por tratarse de una fecha tan significativa en la historia de nuestra civilización, el premio será otorgado en una ceremonia oficial que contará con la asistencia de las figuras más destacadas del siglo. Le rogamos nos haga llegar a vuelta de correo la lista de sus invitados personales. Debido a razones de seguridad no deberán exceder el número de sus años, es decir cincuenta.

Reiterándole mis felicitaciones en mi nombre y el de las empresas que auspician este evento, quedo a sus órdenes.

Licenciado Mario T. de la Campa

Estimado Licenciado de la Campa:

Le agradezco la notificación sobre mi premio y aprovecho para enviar afectuosos saludos a todos aquellos que hayan contribuído para que este sueño se realice. He meditado largamente sobre la lista de mis invitados especiales y finalmente he logrado reducirla a cincuenta y cinco. Son tantas las personas a quienes desearía beneficiar con la pompa y el brillo del festejo que esta no fue una tarea fácil. Espero que el número un poco más elevado no les ocasione mayores inconvenientes. Después de todo ¿qué dilema más feliz que el de tener demasiados amigos?

Cordialmente,

Violeta S. Caruso
Profesora de Piano

Srta. Violeta S. Caruso:

Por la presente le hago saber que el día 31 de diciembre de 1999, después de las numerosas quejas recibidas por el vecindario, su inmueble será clausurado como se estipula en el reglamento

# The Contest

Dear Miss Caruso:

Please accept our warm congratulations for having been the winner of the contest "31st of December 1999." This year, since the date is of such significance in the history of our civilization, the prize will be awarded at an official ceremony with some of the most outstanding figures of the century in attendance. We request that you send us by return mail the list of your personal guests. For reasons of security, it should not exceed the number of your years, that is, fifty.

Again, my own congratulations along with those of the organizations sponsoring this event, I am at your service.

Mario T. de la Campa, Esq.

Dear Mr. de la Campa:

Thank you for the notification of my prize and I will also use this occasion to send fond greetings to all those who have contributed so that this dream may be realized. I have thought long and hard over the list of my special guests and have finally reduced the number to fifty-five. There are so many people I would like to be able to enjoy all the pomp and brilliance of the celebration that limiting the list was not an easy task. I hope that the slightly higher number will not be a major inconvenience for you. After all, what happier dilemma than to have too many friends?

Sincerely,

Violeta S. Caruso
Piano teacher

Miss Violeta S. Caruso:

This is to inform you that on the 31st of December 1999, after the numerous complaints received by the neighborhood, your apartment will be sealed as stipulated in the city

concerniente a la manutención sanitaria de la vivienda en este municipio.

Le rogamos nuevamente que limpie los desperdicios amontonados a la entrada de su domicilio y le reiteramos, por última vez, que no se permiten más de dos animales por inmueble. Los agentes que se presentarán en la fecha estipulada tiene órdenes de deshacerse del excedente inmediatamente.

Sin más,

Fernando R. Martínez
Subjefe
Sanidad Municipal

—◇—

Estimada Srta. Caruso:

De mi mayor consideración:

Le rogamos atenerse a las reglas del Concurso y restringir su lista de amigos participantes a cincuenta, cincuenta y uno, al máximo dado que se avecina la fecha de su cumpleaños. De lo contrario, nos será imposible hacer la entrega del premio.

Cordialmente,

María M. de Rossi
Secretaria Técnica
Concurso Viaje del Milenio

—◇—

Jueves, 31 de diciembre de 1999

## Diario El Provincial

SOCIALES

Esta tarde, a las 16 horas, las Damas de la Sociedad Numismática y Geográfica entregarán el premio del Concurso Viaje del Milenio consistente de un viaje en globo a la ganadora, Srta. Violeta S. Caruso. Como es ya tradicional, la ceremonia se llevará a cabo delante de la casa de la premiada para promover el interés en la geografía y la numismática en la población. La Sra. Matilde Díaz de Kleinman pronunciará el discurso de entrega.

—◇—

ordinances concerning the sanitary maintenance of living quarters.

We ask you again to clear away the trash piled at the entrance to your dwelling and we repeat, for the last time, that no more than two animals are allowed per unit. The police who will appear on the stipulated date are under orders to remove all excess animals immediately.

That is all for now,

Fernando R. Martínez
Assistant Director
City Sanitation Department

Dear Miss Caruso:

With greatest consideration:
We request that you adhere to the rules of the contest and restrict your list of participating friends to fifty, fifty-one at the most given that the date of your birth is approaching. Otherwise, it will be impossible for us to present the prize.

Sincerely,

María M. de Rossi
Technical Secretary
Voyage of the Millennium Contest

Thursday, December 31, 1999

## *The Provincial Daily*

SOCIETY NEWS

This afternoon at four o'clock the Ladies of the Nuismatic and Geographical Society will present the prize of the Voyage of the Millennium Contest, consisting of a balloon trip, to the winner, Miss Violeta S. Caruso. In keeping with the tradition, the ceremony will take place before the house of the prizewinner to arouse interest on the part of the neighborhood in nuismatic science and geography. Miss Matilde Díaz de Kleinman will give the address preceding the presentation of the award.

Viernes, 1 de enero de 2000

## *El Indagador*

### Arrójase al vacío con sus gatos despúes
### de implorar por su suerte

En un desarrollo que dejó atónitos a participantes y vecinos, la ganadora del Concurso Viaje del Milenio se arrojó del globo que debía llevarla al hotel donde se la hospedaría a la espera del barco en el cual realizaría la vuelta al mundo. Al parecer, la imposibilidad de viajar con todos sus gatos y el desalojo de su vivienda debido a condiciones insalubres motivó este gesto desesperado.

*(Fotos en el rotograbado de nuestra edición especial este domingo. ¡No se la pierda!)*

## *The Investigator*

DAILY NEWS

### Throws herself overboard with her cats
### after pleading for her fate

In a development that left participants and neighbors stunned, the winner of the Voyage of the Millennium Contest threw herself from the balloon that was to take her to the hotel where she was to board the ship for the round-the-world voyage. It appears that since it was impossible for her to travel with all her cats and she had been evicted from her home due to unsanitary conditions she was driven to this desperate act.

*(Photographs in the illustrated section of our special edition on Sunday. Don't miss it!)*

# Dios los creó y ellos se juntaron

*La tentación de verte me ha hecho venir a esta casa en lugar de esperar tu próxima carta. No aguanto más esta separación de vecinos colindantes y tu decisión de encerrarte me parece injusta. Todos tenemos el derecho de conocer a la persona a quien le hemos confiado los secretos más profundos de nuestra existencia. Es cierto que soy demasiado chica para tener verdaderos secretos, como los tuyos o los de mi mamá que siempre habla en voz baja. Es cierto que tal vez no te interese ver a una colegiala preocupada por las notas que le pone la maestra en sus composiciones pero, por favor, es preciso que leas la carta que te he puesto personalmente bajo la puerta porque el cartero ya no nos sirve y quiero saber y que sepas la verdad.*

Protestó y se desgañitó la viejita disfrazada de nena. Exigió que le abrieran la puerta, que la dejaran pasar. El vecino amnistiado se había acogido a una vida retirada. No quiso salir de su encierro. Estaba cómodo rodeado de sus recuerdos más queridos, las tarjetas postales, la medalla con la cruz gamada, las fotos de cuando entraba sin pedir permiso en la casa de gobierno. No miraba televisión, no le interesaban las nenas y mucho menos las viejitas de apellido extranjero que cada vez se ponían más corajudas, más hinchapelotas. Lástima, porque nosotros queremos verles las caras antes de que sea demasiado tarde.

# Birds of a Feather

*The temptation to see you has brought me to this house instead of waiting for your next letter. Being next-door neighbors I can no longer bear this separation and your decision to shut yourself up seems unfair to me. We all have the right to know the person to whom we've confided the deepest secrets of our lives. It's true that I'm just a girl, too young to have real secrets, like yours and those of my mama who always talks in a low voice. It's true that perhaps it doesn't interest you to see a schoolgirl worried about the grades she gets on her papers, but please, it's important that you read this letter that I'm putting under your door myself because the postman is no longer of any use to us and I want you to know the truth.*

The little old lady disguised as a girl protested and screamed. She demanded that they open the door and let her in. The neighbor, a man who'd been granted amnesty, welcomed the secluded life. He had no desire to leave his confinement. He was comfortable surrounded by his most treasured mementos, the postcards, the medal with the swastika, the photos from the time he was free to enter the presidential mansion whenever he pleased. He never watched televison, had no interest in little girls and much less in old ladies with foreign surnames who kept getting more and more irate, more and more a pain in the butt. A shame, because we'd like to see what they are all about before it's too late.

# ¿Te comunicaste?

Por teléfono me lo dijo porque no podía hacerlo directamente. Es un cobarde que no entiende la mitad de lo que le pasa. Estaba nerviosa por lo de mi tía y cuando él me vino con esa novedad le canté cuarenta verdades y no me guardé ninguna de las informaciones exclusivas de su prima de la provincia. Creo que debe de haber necesitado sentarse. Hubo un silencio sepulcral del otro lado de la línea y después esa canción que habla de cuando una pareja se va a reunir en el cielo. Fue entonces que me dió el ataque de risa. Empezó de a poco pero me tenté y cuando él, que evidentemente había dejado el teléfono descolgado con la radio puesta, se me presentó de cuerpo y alma en el departamento; me saltaban las lágrimas a raudales y me debo haber hecho pis encima porque lo de espérame en el cielo, corazón, me había despertado como una cosquillita interna, unas ganas de rascarme, bailar la raspa de adentro para afuera y es así que él empezó con lo de tomarme el pulso y yo meta a las carcajadas y las lágrimas porque se me atragantó la risa y me quedé con la boca abierta y olí mi propio pis que había formado un charco que a él seguramente le daba asco porque desde siempre ha sido un muchacho medio relamido y es lo que todavía me sigue gustando porque no hay nada más lindo que un tipo que sepa cómo comer masitas de crema sin enchastrarse los dedos, que te traiga flores para los aniversarios y que vaya paquete, con ropa oscura, a los entierros de tus parientes sobre todo ahora con la enfermedad de mi tía y con los problemas que trae la tercera edad cuando la gente no se cuida como debe. Siempre me ha gustado ese aspecto de su personalidad, así que las boberías me las aguantaba porque para qué necesita una alguien que cobre un sueldo alto o que quiera buscar empleo o que le sea fiel estilo perrito faldero si la persona no es presentable. Como hombre, es un accesorio perfecto. Iba bien con toda mi ropa y por la diferencia de edad hasta me hacía parecer más joven. Para contestar a tu pregunta, no, no me da vergüenza lo del colchón de goma ni tampoco extraño la casa, eso sí me gustaría que pidas que me pongan teléfono en la habitación por si tiene algo más que decirme.

# Did You Get Through?

He told me on the phone because he couldn't do it to my face. He's a coward who doesn't understand half of what's happening right under his nose. I was nervous because of the business with my aunt and when he comes out with that news I gave him a piece of my mind and didn't spare any of the inside information I had about his cousin, the girl who lives in the sticks. I think that must have knocked him back on his heels. There was a dead silence on the other end of the line and then that old tune about a couple who will be reunited in heaven. That gave me an attack of the giggles. It started slowly but I was tempted and when it was clear he'd left the phone off the hook and the radio playing, I presented myself in living color in his apartment. I was crying buckets and must have peed on top of that because that business of waiting for me in heaven, my dear, that really made my blood boil, I felt like scratching, I was seething and that's when he began to take my pulse and me in the middle of laughing and crying except I was choking from laughter and was left gasping and smelled my own piss that had formed a puddle that he certainly found disgusting because he's always been quite proper and that's what I still like about him because there's nothing nicer than a guy who knows how to eat cream puffs without getting his fingers all sticky, who brings you flowers for anniversaries, and who, what a bore, goes dressed in black to the funerals of all your relatives, above all now with my aunt's illness and with the problems that come with the third age when people don't take care of themselves they way they should. I've always liked that aspect of his personality, so I put up with the nonsense because why does a woman need some guy who earns a high salary or who wants to find a job or will be as faithful as a lap dog if he's not presentable. As a man, he's the perfect accessory. He went well with all my clothes and the difference in age only made me look younger. But to answer your question, no, I'm not ashamed of the foam rubber mattress nor do I miss the house, but I would like you to ask them to put a telephone in my room in case he has something more to say to me.

# Te acompaño en el sentimiento

—si te da no sé qué no te lo pongas porque la experiencia indica que hay momentos en los cuales se establece un desacuerdo entre la ocasión y un vestido. Entonces hay como un silencio que se te forma alrededor del cuerpo y ni siquiera vale la pena hablar porque sabes que la gente no te escucha     prefieren mirarte la barriga o un fleco que cae donde menos hace falta.

—a mi tía yo la miraba en detalle, despacito. Me fijaba en un rulo que le quedaba detrás de la oreja, en el brillo de un pulóver beige entretejido con hilitos dorados y fijáte que ahora que me gustaría imitarla no puedo reproducirle el gesto ese . . .

—sólo de escuchar cómo hablan empiezo a imaginarme cosas marrones, flores mustias, calcomanías de pájaros y mariposas en los azulejos de una cocina con olor a fritura donde alguien acaba de lavar la sartén de las milanesas.

cállense la boca viejas chotas que quiero pensar en cosas modernas, ir a un bowling, comprarme un pasaje de ida y vuelta en un crucero con todo incluído, sobre todo la copa de champaña en la mesa del capitán antes de bailar una de esas piezas con letras obscenas donde te aconsejan que te muevas y te sacudas y te menees     cómo me gusta cómo me calienta reconocer esas partes del cuerpo, ¿les pasó alguna vez no saber a qué se referían? pero a quién le estoy hablando si ustedes ni siquiera deben tener partes del cuerpo     todo les duele al por mayor     cállense la boca despabílense que no por ir al cementerio para acompañarlas porque yo no creo en estas cosas que no por ir al cementerio debo poner cara y voz de circunstancias.

—dale, servíte un caramelo y cantáme esa melodía tan alegre que te oí el otro día. Era en inglés, no? Se te nota el entusiasmo cuando pronuncias.

# You Have My Sympathy

—if they give you anything at all don't put it on because experience shows that there are moments when a mismatch occurs between the occasion and the clothes. Then something like a silence forms around the body and it's no use even to open your mouth because you know that nobody will listen to you—they prefer to look at your belly or a fleck that falls on the exact wrong spot.

—I would look my aunt over in detail, very slowly. I would concentrate on a curl behind her ear, or the glint of a beige sweater with little gold threads interwoven and imagine that now I'd like to imitate her but I just can't reproduce that certain gesture . . .

—only by listening I start imagining brown things, faded flowers, decals of birds and butterflies on the tiles of a kitchen that smells of grease where someone has just finished washing the frying pan after making meatballs.

oh shut up you old dummies I want to think of up-to-date things, go bowling, buy myself a round-trip ticket for a cruise with everything included especially the glass of champagne at the captain's table before dancing one of those pieces with obscene lyrics where they tell you to move it and shake it whatever you feel like          how hot I get noticing those parts of my body          do they sometimes not know what they're referring to? but why am I talking to you if you don't even have body parts          everything hurts the whole ball of wax shut up and smell the coffee          don't think that just 'cause I'm going with you to the cemetery to keep you company 'cause I don't believe in such things just 'cause I'm going with you to the cemetery I should put on a face and voice to suit the occasion.

—come on, have a candy and sing me that very cheerful tune I heard you belt out the other day. It was in English, right? One can feel the enthusiasm the way you pronounced it.

# bien mirado, se le parece

*para Virgilio Piñera*

La memoria se le había atascado en ese instante. Veía a su perro cruzar la calle, despedirse con un suspiro y desaparecer después en los brazos de una mujer de uñas largas y pelo rubio. *No vayas,* tendría que haberle rogado. *Volvé,* gritarle acaso, aunque lo atropellara un auto. La rubia debía de haber ido a la carnicería porque se veían los paquetes medio ensangrentados por la ventana de atrás, desparramándose ante la voraz acometida que deshacía los envoltorios con dentelladas nada tímidas, desmentidos de su pasado de faldero. Perro de departamento vuelto fiera. Se dio un festín. A él sí que todo esto le cayó bien, porfiaría ella asegurando: *no, no conocía a la rubia, nada sé del cuerpo, no, no reconozco al finado, ¿así que ella dice que había sido mi novio?*

24

# well yes at second glance
# he looks just like him

*for Virgilio Piñera*

Her memory was stuck in that brief moment. She saw the dog cross the street and plunge into the arms of the long-nailed blonde without hesitation. Don't go, she should have pleaded with him. Come back scream even if it meant he could have been hit by a car. It looked like the blonde had been to the butcher's what with all those bloody packages barely shielded by the rear window as they opened up and scattered all around        who could have guessed it the cute little lap dog let himself go        was having a feast, unstoppable, in a frenzy, biting in every direction. It figures: any day a meek apartment doggie may turn into the wildest beast. At least he got something good out of all of this what a banquet. No, she reassured them, time and again, *I didn't know the blonde        and as for the dismembered body, terrible, isn't it? There's nothing I could tell you, can't identify the poor man's remains, what a liar how the hell does she come off saying he had been my boyfriend?*

# actualidades

En este país hay cuatro gatos locos que se pelean día y noche para que les preste atención un león distraído por unos callos que no le permiten correr detrás de un conejo blanco de piel sedosa y corazoncito rosado que late y late sin saber que un día los gatos advertirán que es su rival y entonces ya se sabe.

# breaking news

In this country there are four crazy cats that fight day and night to get noticed by a lion who's distracted by some calluses that keep him from chasing a white rabbit with silky fur and sweet rosy heart that beats and beats not knowing that one day the cats will catch on that he's their rival and then well you know the rest.

# Jóvenes emprendedores

Frenéticamente trabaja en la construcción de un monumento para su primo menor. No escatima esfuerzos porque sabe que si no lo termina para el día de su cumpleaños le recordará que es un infeliz, le quitará su novia y arruinará para siempre sus posibilidades de ascenso en la firma que un día, presidida por el primo menor, empleará a toda la familia con sueldos irrisorios que se gastarán en magníficos asados para Navidad y año nuevo.

# Up-and-coming
# Young Businessmen

He works frantically on the construction of a monument for his younger cousin. He spares no effort because he knows if he doesn't finish it in time for the cousin's birthday he'll call him a loser, win away his girlfriend, and completely wreck his chances for promotion in the company that one day, presided over by the very same cousin, will employ the whole family, pay them ludicrous wages that they'll blow on fabulous feasts for Christmas and New Year's.

# ¿por qué no escribir una novela en vez de ir al cine o mirar el techo mientras la grasa se te acumula en el centro de la voluntad?

Tiene un pasado turbio. Su abuela, una mujer ostentosamente juvenil y envidiosa que logró robarle sin demasiado esfuerzo una noviecita tímida con quien concurría a un bar del centro atendido por el bisnieto de un coronel del ejército de ocupación de un país limítrofe devastado por la furia de unos vendavales arbitrarios aunque no esporádicos, le dejó un resentimiento en el alma que se manifestaba gástricamente en momentos íntimos. Su padre era un hombre de bigotitos erectos y porte modesto cuyo nada ambiguo oficio hacía preciso vestir de gala a su madre y lucirla en las esquinas.

(Cuando me habla no mide las consecuencias. Sabe que me le entregaré ni bien termine de hacer el inventario pero me falta bastante, así que si alguna de ustedes quiere probar entretanto, adelante.)

# why not write a novel instead of going to the movies or staring at the ceiling while the fat gathers up around the middle of your willpower?

He has a sleazy past. His grandmother, flashy and petty, succeeded without too much trouble in stealing away from him a cute and shy little bride with whom he used to go to a downtown bar managed by the grandson of the colonel of a bordering country devastated by the fury of certain arbitrary but not sporadic whirlwinds and so he was left feeling a bitterness in his soul that surfaced gastrically during intimate moments. His father was a man of modest bearing and a moustache turned up at the ends whose totally unambiguous job made it necessary to deck out his mother in fancy clothes and show her off on street corners.

(When he talks to me he doesn't think of the consequences. He knows I'll give in to him the minute I finish taking the inventory but it will take me quite a while yet, so if any of you want to have a go in the meantime, be my guest.)

# pan al que no quiere dientes

Había tantas flacas en esa ciudad que los hombres andaban con frío en el alma añorando la almohada de pechos acogedores y generosos en vez de la agresividad de vaginas abiertas y disponibles sin un solo milímetro de grasa interpuesto. El excesivo entusiasmo de sus mujeres y amantes por los ejercicios físicos y la terapia anticulinaria los había convertido en cantantes de boleros, profesores de tango y maestros de declamación con la esperanza de abrir los apetitos de tantas minas huesudas. Fernanda, imponente, caderuda, con un acné que hablaba de la lujuria de sus glándulas sebáceas, se impuso en menos de diez minutos.

Las envidiosas escribieron artículos sobre el escándalo de sus rollos y de la vulgaridad de su aliento cargado de frituras y repostería. Se equivocaban porque naturalmente Fernanda no tenía tiempo para los arrumacos de esos hombres insatisfechos. Era meramente la primera en la invasión que se avecinaba ya que había cundido la noticia de que los hábitos dietéticos de esa ciudad habían creado un paraíso con los chocolates y las tortas más baratas del universo.

Ustedes se creen que esta es la historia de los triunfos de Fernanda pero no sean ingenuos que en este mundo nada pasa como suponemos. Los hombres sueñan con ella pero las flacas esconden la comida y dejan que se pudra para usarla como abono y cultivar unas flores atrevidas, carnosas que aguantan viento, frío, nevadas y te siguen jodiendo la vida las cuatro estaciones del año.

# as welcome as a hole in the head

There were so many skinny women in that city that the men went around with shriveled hearts yearning for the pillow of welcoming and generous breasts instead of the open and available vaginas with not a single millimeter of fat in between. The excessive enthusiasm of their wives and lovers for physical exercise and anticulinary therapy had turned them into bolero singers, teachers of tango and of declamation in hopes of opening the appetite of so many bony chicks. Fernanda, imposing, big-hipped, with acne showing the lustiness of her sebaceous glands, took over in less than ten minutes.

The envious women wrote articles about her scandalous rolls of fat and her vulgar breath smelling of fried food and rich pastries. They were mistaken because naturally Fernanda had no time for the sweet talk of those unsatisfied men. She was merely the first of an invasion approaching since news spread that the dietary habits of that city had created a paradise with the cheapest chocolates and pies in the world.

You think this is the story of Fernanda's triumphs but don't be naive for in this world nothing comes out the way we think it will. The men dream of her but the skinny ones hide the food and let it rot to use as fertilizer to cultivate bold flowers—fleshy, able to withstand wind, cold, snow—and keep screwing up your life all four seasons of the year.

# ¿Qué me pongo?

—me visto de reina y después, ya arreglada, nadie me va a sacar el cetro.

—pero así no vale, las reinas nacen; no es algo que puedas inventar con la ropa.

—me visto de militar y entro a dispararle a todo el mundo

—te prefiero princesa porque entonces nos van a sacar fotos jugando al tenis y por ahí nos regalan las raquetas

—si no me tuviera que depilar las piernas me desvestiría de santa y les helaría la sangre. Así como me ves.

# What Should I Wear?

—I'll just dress up as a queen, and when I'm all fixed up, nobody will dare snatch the throne away from me.

—but that's not the way it works, queens are born, you can't just decide to be one and fake it with clothes.

—I'll dress in an army uniform and burst through the door shooting at everybody

—I'd rather have you be a princess because then they'll take photos of us playing tennis and maybe they'll even let us keep the rackets

—if I didn't have to shave my legs I'd undress like a saint and make their blood run cold. Just like that.

# pajaritos en la cabeza

Tengo que resolver un asunto urgente en la cancillería, así que te ruego que cuentes inmediatamente el número de canarios que hemos dejado entrar al país y llenes los formularios azules que colocarás en la gaveta de los marrones y dejarás cerrados a doble llave. Con respecto al deceso prematuro del gorrión no hay que decir nada ya que cualquiera de las calandrias se travestirá sin que nadie se dé cuenta y podrá sobrellevar los rigores del concierto. Te deseo un feliz fin de semana, nos veremos el lunes ya que mi gestión será muy exitosa, palomita, y trinaremos, gorgueros llenos de alpiste y alegría.

# bats in the belfry

Got to go take care of an urgent matter in the Consulate        so please I beg you        count right away the number of canaries we've allowed into the country, fill out the blue forms and double-lock them in the drawer with the brown certificates. As far as the premature death of the sparrow let's not breathe as much as a syllable any nightingale can perform his role and the concert will proceed without a hitch. I wish you a great weekend, till Monday then my dear turtledove        my business deal will go swimmingly and I just know that you and I will be chirping away in no time        our bellies filled with food and delight.

# de película

A mi casa vino de visita una adolescente envejecida de culo caído y mirada indudablemente distraída debido a una excesiva familiaridad con el álgebra. Me trajo estos bombones que como en silencio frente al televisor porque me ha impuesto una condena de tres horas y cincuenta y cinco minutos para que me concentre en su destino y descubra entre los avisos de perfumes y detergentes una suciedad que todavía la frena y le enturbia el deseo. Quiere enamorarse de un joven jugador de beisbol de mejillas coloradas y pelo corto pero hasta ahora sólo ha logrado odiarlo y como se avecina la fecha en que deben casarse no puede esperar el momento en que como la chica en la serie que estoy mirando, nos hará guiñaditas toda vestida de blanco.

# out of sight

She came to visit me at my house, a teenager with a sagging behind and a distracted look due to knowing too much algebra. She
brought me these candies that I eat in silence in front of the TV because she has sentenced me to three hours and fifty-five minutes so
that I may concentrate on her future and discover among the ads for
perfumes and detergents something dirty that still holds her back
and muddies her desire. She wants to fall in love with a young baseball player with red cheeks and short hair but as of now she's only
come so far as to hate him and since their wedding date is closing in
she can't wait for the moment when like the girl in the sitcom I'm
watching she'll wink and wave at us, dressed in white head to toe.

# ¿no te resulta cara conocida?

lo que más rabia me da es que cuando camina me pisa los talones     y entonces se me seca la boca de sólo pensar que faltan dos o tres segundos para que haga lo de siempre y no quiera cruzar miradas. Pasa adelante, la vista fija en la vereda de enfrente como si no existiera porque qué le importan todos esos cafés, nuestras espléndidas noches en camas revueltas, los encuentros en esta misma estación de tren a la cual va ahora indudablemente para llegar a su casa y acaso aún le queden algunas botellas de ese vino que compramos a mitad de precio     me da rabia verle los zoquetes de color equivocado y sobre todo su pasarme desde tan cerca sin saber que pronto alguien abrirá el sobre y con manos agitadas y casi sin aliento le mostrará una foto, una llave, nuestro escándalo.

# haven't I seen that face before?

what really gets me is when he walks behind me so close he could step on my heels I tell you my mouth goes dry just thinking about it        as always he is about to walk past me without as much as a glance. He walks by, stares across the street as though I wasn't there        what does he care about our midday escapades the splendid nights        carelessly abandoned beds our hushed conversations in the train station, the same one he is going to now        I am sure he is heading home although we didn't even go through half the excellent bottles of wine I got for us at a discount. I can't stand it when I catch a glimpse of his mismatched socks and above all the way in which he hurries        so close        indifferent and arrogant without knowing that soon she will open up the envelope and breathless, shocked, will confront him with the photograph, an address, a key, our scandal.

# más fuerte que la hiedra
## a la pared

me importa más que pierda y por eso la trato mejor de lo que se
merece
me importa sobre todo que mañana venga a visitarme con un ramo
de rosas
yo tendré la cola entre las piernas          pero aún así olerá mi triunfo
y casi sin que nadie se dé cuenta depositará sus espinas a la salida del
observatorio

# I've got you under my skin

I'd rather see her lose so I treat her better than she deserves
what's important to me above all is that she come back to visit me
tomorrow rose bouquet in hand
I'll have my tail between my legs          even so I just know she'll
smell my success
and almost without anybody noticing I bet she'll put down her
thorns at the exit of the observatory

# no me jodas

Fernando ha traído dos mujeres a la fiesta pero como lo han dejado solo él se ha puesto a pensar en cosas tristes del pasado. En el instante preciso en que empieza a darle vueltas al día de su primera comunión advierte que un dirigente sindical que lo ha venido siguiendo se ha sentado con sus dos amigas y juntos están urdiendo los detalles de una huelga que acabará para siempre con sus negocios. Fernando, ofendido, se acerca y le da una bofetada al dirigente sindical. Las mujeres lanzan una carcajada tintineante mientras numerosos periodistas sacan fotos y echan a correr el rumor de una huelga general para protestar la agresión contra el sindicalista. Es aquí que empieza la historia íntima de Fernando el revolucionario, el desconfiado melancólico que deposita bombas devastadoras en casitas con jardín al frente donde invariablemente hay un futuro torturador lustrándose los borceguíes.

# you must be kidding

Fernando has brought two women to the fiesta but since they've left him alone he has started to think about sad things from way back when. At the very moment he begins to think about the day of his first communion, he notices that a union leader who followed him to the fiesta is now sitting at a table with his two girl friends plotting a strike that will put him out of business forever. Fernando, incensed, goes over and slaps him. The women explode with laughter as a bunch of journalists snap pictures to start the rumor of a general strike to protest the aggression against their union leader. Fernando's uplifting story as the revolutionary, suspicious, and melancholic militant we know starts here as he plants bomb after bomb in white picket-fenced houses occupied by domesticated torturers who are invariably polishing their boots with loving care.

# amantes

Por ese hombre ella se lustra un lunar lechoso que tiene en la pierna derecha. Por esa ruina él trabaja de día en un kiosko de revistas y de noche en un estacionamiento semi vacío al cual sólo vienen parejas deseosas de ocultar la cara antes de escurrirse, huidizas, por la puerta que da directamente al hotel alojamiento. Los domingos salen del brazo y sé que son felices porque ella le ha planchado la camisa blanca y él pasa otra vez sin saludarme sin darle ni siquiera un pedacito de chocolate a un chico con quien voy a todos lados y que de carambola ha heredado esos pelos que le salen de la nariz          pensar que en una época yo le porfiaba que me gustaban aunque seguro se fue porque me habrá visto el asco en los ojos o acaso en las cejas que es donde más se nos nota.

# lovers

It is for him that she polishes a milky mole on her right leg. For that wreck of a woman, he works by day at a magazine stand and by night at a half-empty parking lot where only furtive couples come, eager to hide their faces before they scurry nervously through the doors that lead directly to the hotel. Sundays they go out arm in arm and I know how happy they are because she has ironed his white shirt and he passes me by without saying hello again without giving so much as a bite of chocolate to a young boy I take with me everywhere. As if by chance the kid has inherited from him those nasty little hairs that stick out of his nose. Oh, when I think of how I used to insist ages ago that I loved them. I'm sure he must have seen the disgust in my eyes or maybe right between the eyebrows where everyone can tell.

# andá a saber cuándo te hará falta un favor

Treinta veces tocó la campanilla. Es el príncipe cartero que viene con regalos de fiestas patrióticas. Treinta veces y nadie le contesta. En esta casa son demasiado ricos. No les interesa abrir la puerta a mensajeros groseros, con preocupaciones de guerras e impuestos. Están adentro porque tienen miedo de irse de vacaciones. Juegan a la oca, el monte y apuestan a las carreras por teléfono. Los niños saben que con padres así serán pobres. Por eso salen por la puerta de atrás y adulan a los carteros con caramelos y monedas de oro.

# you never know when you'll need a favor

He rang the bell thirty times. He is the prince-postman bearing patriotic gifts. Thirty times and no answer. They are too wealthy in this house. No interest in opening up the door to vulgar messengers worried about wars and taxes. They remain indoors because they are afraid to go on vacation. They play monopoly, poker, and make bets on the phone. Their kids just know that with parents like that they'll be poor. That's why they come out the back door and bribe the postmen with candy and gold coins.

# tarde o temprano a todos les llega la hora

El faraón se comía las uñas delante de sus hijos y les daba un muy mal ejemplo porque debían aprender a robar sus alimentos de los esclavos improductivos que merodeaban en terrenos baldíos. Pero los esclavos no eran tan idiotas como parecían y cuando jugaban a las cartas se repartían cada piedra del palacio de modo que cuando el faraón fue prolijamente momificado lo único que le quedaba en la vida era la esperanza de que le volvieran a crecer las uñas.

# sooner or later they'll
# have to go

Pharaoh bit and ate his nails in front of his own children setting a very bad example for them because they had to learn on their own how to steal food from the unproductive slaves hanging out in the surrounding vacant lots. But the slaves were not as stupid as they looked and when they played cards they dealt themselves each of the palace stones one by one so that when Pharaoh was neatly mummified the only hope left for him was that his nails would continue to grow.

# yo soy un hombre sincero

—Le pediste que te limpiara el culo de mala manera, por eso te contestó así.

—no era cuestión de ofenderla, sólo de indicarle hasta qué punto yo me la imaginaba en todo detalle

—algo de malo debe de haber visto en tu invitación sobre todo si hasta te bajaste los pantalones

—a las minas les gusta que les hables delicado, que les hagas cositas

—y flores

　　nada de estas historias de bebé　　　decirle mamita

—muy equivocado　　　lo del culo es muy de machote y hasta pensaba pegarle

—de eso nunca hay que hablar porque desvirtúa el romance

—me parece que te va a llamar por teléfono, sobre todo si le mandaste una carta explicándole el asunto de que no dormís y le das vuelta a la cosa todos los días y que ya no te alimentás para no sentirte tan solo sin ella después y el agujero que te ha dejado y lo de la sinceridad y cómo un día de estos vas y le pegas un tiro antes de irte a la pizzería con la prima recién venida de la provincia, esa sí que se las trae, bocona y lista para unas cuantas cosas que ni vos te imaginás.

# I'm just a simple man

—You really insisted that she wipe your ass, that's why she answered you the way she did.

—it wasn't meant to offend her, only to show how I imagined her in every detail

—she must have seen something bad in your invitation especially since you went so far as to lower your pants

—girls like you to talk nice to them, to pet them

—bring flowers
     no acting like a baby calling them mommy

—completely wrong the business of the ass it's caveman stuff and she even thought about hitting you

—this is something one shouldn't ever talk about it spoils any romance

—I think she'll call you, especially if you sent her a letter explaining that you can't sleep and mulling the whole thing over all day every day and now don't even eat so as not to feel so lonely without her afterwards and the hole she has left in you and that business of being sincere and how one of these days you'll shoot her before going to the pizzeria with the cousin just in from the country, now yes she's really a handful, loud-mouthed and ready for some things that even you cannot imagine.

# Descuento

Primero le rebajó dos centavos pero cuando vió su entusiasmo le aumentó cuatro pesos, cosa que ella aceptó inmediatamente y lo vendió enseguida sin campaña publicitaria con un margen de ganancia del cuatrocientos por ciento. Mientras los habitantes del mercado envejecían, el objeto aumentaba de precio hasta que llegamos nosotros que no entendemos el idioma, fusilamos a todos los comerciantes y nos dedicamos a pulir y pulir el objeto entonces él nos devolvió la sonrisa, reflejó el rulito que tenemos en la frente y nos dejó chochos, olvidados de que nos había rebanado la mitad del cuerpo para que rodemos mejor.

# Bargain Hunters Beware

First he lowered the price two cents but upon seeing her glee he raised it four dollars which she accepted right away only to sell immediately without even advertising at a four-hundred-percent gain. The market's inhabitants grew older as the value of the object skyrocketed, that's when we came in without any understanding of their language and, unhampered by their quaint customs, we proceeded to shoot all the businessmen and devoted ourselves to polishing the object until it smiled back at us, reflected our lovable curls, and made us oh so happy and oblivious to the fact that it had carved our body in halves so we could roll down with ease.

# canta como un ángel

es una canalla que me mira de reojo cuando le digo mi serenata
es una loca emplumada que no me retribuye los arrumacos
pero cuando unto un pan con mermelada me persigue trina que te
trina insistente como si a mí me siguiera importando ahora que ya
me compré una radio y me llevo mi musiquita a los picnics y no
necesito más de su incómodo batir de alas tijeretazo
mina revirada tejiendo calceta

# sings like an angel

she is a bitch who looks at me with suspicion when offer my love
songs
she is scatterbrained     all feathers and sequins indifferent and cold
but when she sees me sit down     put jelly on my bread     she
comes     she comes chirping away insistently as though I still
cared     now that I bought a cd player and I can take my own music
to picnics who needs the uncomfortable batting of her scissored
wings?
crazy broad stewing in her own juice

# ¿qué le sirvo? ¿desea algo más?

El lobo que quería comer a hansel y gretel se ocultó en el bosque porque tenía miedo de perderse y terminar en la ciudad. Fue entonces que vio a caperucita roja y huyó aterrorizado ante tanto colorado, tanta capucha que le recordaba su horrible experiencia con marlene dietrich. Entró por la primera puerta que encontró y ya en la cama disfrazado de abuelita imitó a un lobo para que caperucita no se lo llevara con ella a trabajar en un palacio lleno de animalitos domésticos y esclavos porque este era una bestia realmente bestia que ni siquiera sabía la diferencia entre la latifundista bella durmiente y una caperucita de mala muerte, dominguera, demasiado limpia para satisfacer el apetito que le hacía bailar las tripas y cagarse de miedo.

# what may I bring you?
# would you like anything else?

The wolf that wanted to eat hansel and gretel hid in the woods because he was afraid of getting lost and ending up in the city. It was then he saw little red riding hood and fled horrified by so much red and a hood that reminded him of a dreadful experience he'd had with marlene dietrich. He dashed into the first door he found and there on the bed disguised as a harmless old grandmother he played wolf so little red riding hood wouldn't take him with her to work in a palace filled with pet animals and slaves because this was a beast really a beast that didn't even know the difference between a plantation sleeping beauty and a cheesy little red riding hood all dressed up in her Sunday best, too clean to satisfy the kind of appetite that made his gut sing and scared him shitless.

# se te fue la mano, che

Dos regalos le hizo. Ella sintió que debía mostrárselos inmediatemente a su novio para que él la quisiera más pero a él se le ocurrió que lo mejor era cambiar de frecuencia y usurpó su lugar. Por eso ella ahora se come los codos mientras ellos van al cine, cenan a la luz de la luna y un día de estos hasta se animan a bailar al son de un bandoneón.

# you went too far, you know

He gave her two presents. She felt she should show them to her sweetheart right away so he would love her more but he got the idea it was time to jump ship and took her place. That's why she's now left high and dry while they go to the movies, dine by the light of the moon, and one of these days they'll even get up the courage to dance when the accordion plays.

# es un sistema bárbaro

saben cómo organizarse
marchan con un ritmo armónico porque ni se aman ni se odian
con gusto les doy mis ganancias
administradores exclusivos
albaceas que acrecientan mi deuda y se la cobran largo látigo en el
centro de todas mis semanas

# terrific system

they know how to get organized
they march in perfect harmony because they feel neither love nor
hate for one another
gladly I give them all I make
my very own administrators
executors who increase my debt and week after week come, whip in
hand, to collect

# ese hombre es un espectáculo

—el boleto me lo regaló una tarde en que yo estaba sentada como siempre frente al espejo sacándome los pelitos del mentón que siempre me empiezan a crecer a eso de las cuatro y a la hora de la merienda ya me embroman de lo lindo cuando me paso la mano como quien no quiere la cosa

—entonces habrá venido más temprano de la seccional, no? porque ahora que le arreglamos el asunto de la noche y puede cobrarse su premio con los pibes de la droga es un sacrificio económico      lo de pasar por la casa a la tarde      habrá querido darte una sorpresa, alegrarte la vida que te hace falta siempre métale que le meta a la televisión

—el boleto me lo regaló una tarde en que yo estaba sentada como siempre frente al espejo
y se reflejaba la ventana y vos estabas con esa pollera de flecos, la mano metida adentro de la bombacha y te vi mirándonos te ví alegrarte porque estabas segura de que me iría y los dejaría solos      hija de puta      azafata de mala muerte      te ví
y te lo refriego en la cara      a mí también me gusta quedarme
y mirarlos por la ventana      a mí también me gusta por eso le he comprado calzoncillos rayados      por eso te lo regalo empaquetado      pelotudo de mis pesadillas.

# that man is something else

—he gave me the ticket one afternoon when I was sitting as usual in front of the mirror tweezing those hairs on my chin that always start to grow around four and already bother me by snack time when I rub my chin as though by chance

—then he must have left the office earlier, right? because now that we figured out the night's business for him so he can collect from the crackheads it's a financial loss to come by the house in the afternoon he must have wanted to surprise you, cheer you up which you need always sitting in front of the television

—he gave me the ticket one afternoon when I was sitting as usual in front of the mirror
and it reflected the window and you were wearing that dotted sweater, hand inside the panties and I saw you looking at us I saw you cheer up because you were sure I'd go and leave you two alone son-of-a-bitching loser of a stewardess I saw you and I rub your face in it I would also like to stay and watch them through the window I'd like that too that's why I've bought you striped underpants     that's why I give them to you all wrapped up     asshole of my nightmares.

# la valija

Estoy de acuerdo, vive en un cuchitril. Y, sin embargo, sale a hacer pinta todas las tardes. Aturdida, con una bandejita de masas en la mano, llega a la casa. Toca el timbre. No ve a la mujer que sale apurada antes de que su amiga baje a abrirle, en batón y chinelas con el cigarrillo colgándole de la boca.

—Mirá que se te hizo tarde. Siempre dale que te dale con la manía de las masitas. Vení. Entrá. Hoy te toca empezar.

Están todas ahí. Las viejitas. Reinas de la belleza en algún lugar de Polonia. Estrellas del gimnasio. Hijas de un rabino       de un tallista       de un mueblero       de un ateo revolucionario       del schatjn y del mendigo, del jazn y del ladrón que desapareció la noche antes de que lo descubrieran. Están todas ahí. Han cobrado la jubilación esa semana y han invertido en té, en ingredientes para hacer las comidas al gusto de entonces. Cuando hablan en idisch algo voraz, exuberante, se escapa en la risa ligera con que festejan chistes sin necesidad de decirlos. Están nerviosas porque son felices.

La dueña de casa ha abierto ya la valija. Ellas, congregadas alrededor suyo, se pelean por este o aquel vestido, el uniforme, hasta la ropa del campo de concentración. Algunos son harapos irreconocibles pero ni bien se los ponen lucen jóvenes, las dentaduras postizas adquieren el brillo de la realidad y con un aire de celebración, de orquesta desgañitada, se imprecan en polaco, alemán, ruso, idisch, se dan órdenes. Bailan.

La portera toca el timbre pero no la oyen. Debe de haber sido por eso que tuvieron que derribar la puerta. Para que entren a desinfectar. Para que se lleven esa valija mugrienta, fuente de cucarachas para todo el edificio. Piantadas. Viejas chotas. Judías de mierda.

# the suitcase

I agree, she lives in a pigsty. And yet she goes out every afternoon to show herself off. In a daze, carrying a tray of cookies, she comes to the house. Rings the bell. She doesn't see the woman who leaves in a great rush before her girlfriend comes down to open the door, in robe and slippers with a cigarette hanging from her lips.
—Listen, you're late. Always the same business with the cookies. Come, come in. Today it's your turn to begin.

They're all here, the little old ladies. Beauty queens from some place in Poland. Gymnastic champions. Daughters of a rabbi a wood carver a cabinetmaker a revolutionary atheist    a jazn and the thief who disappeared the night before they discovered him. They're all here. They've received their pension checks this week and have spent the money on tea and ingredients to make dishes they liked back then. When they speak in Yiddish something voracious, exuberant, escapes in the light laugh with which they enjoy jokes without having to tell them. They're nervous because they're happy.

The hostess has already opened the suitcase. The women crowd around her, fight for this or that dress, the uniform, even the clothes from the concentration camp. Some garments are ragged, unrecognizable but the minute the women put them on they seem young, their dentures gleam like real teeth and with an atmosphere of celebration, of ear-splitting orchestra, they swear in Polish, German, Russian, Yiddish, give orders. Dance.

The concierge rings the bell but they don't hear her. That must be why they had to tear down the door. So they could get in and disinfect the place. So they could carry off that filthy suitcase, the source of cockroaches for the entire building. Nutcakes. Old hags. Shitty Jews.

# mano fuerte

En el país hay una persona retraída que nunca ha ido a ninguna manifestación ni se ha presentado a las reuniones oficiales en que condecoramos a quienes se abstienen de criticarnos. Se trata de alguien que tiene pies planos, no viste ropa adecuada para los deportes que enfrascan a la sana ciudadanía de nuestra nación y demuestra desinterés por las oportunidades comerciales y financieras abiertas por esta espléndida economía planetaria. Una persona que seguramente cantará como un pajarito y nos dirá su secreto al primer apremio, a la segunda o tercera descarga eléctrica en los pies o acaso en la axila que invariablemente les llega al alma.

# a strong hand

He is the country's loner. He has never participated in any demonstrations or attended the official ceremonies in which we decorate those who have never criticized us. He has flat feet, does not even own decent workout clothes to practice the various sports that are the rage among the healthy citizenry of our nation, and, in addition, he is indifferent to the many commercial and financial opportunities available in this splendid global economy. This is somebody who will surely sing like a birdie and tell us his secret at the first push, the second or third electric shock on the feet or perhaps in the armpit, that's the one, I tell you, that goes directly to the soul.

# ¿Quién habrá sido?

Entran en pareja porque les da frío cuando falta el otro. Caminan muy juntos y en el cine no pueden evitar estremecerse con el roce de una pierna, mi brazo. Si no estuvieran yo no podría concentrarme en todo esto pero si se dieran cuenta de que me hacen falta seguro que se irían indignados y a mí la risa se me quedaría atorada, seca, irreconocible.

# Who Could It Have Been?

They come in twos because they feel cold when the other one is missing. They walk close together and cannot but quiver in the movies at the soft touch of one of my legs, an arm. If they were not there, I would be unable to concentrate but if they knew how much I need them, I am sure they would leave immediately, proud, indignant, and then what would I do with this dry, unrecognizable laughter stuck in my throat?

# Por la patria

Había una vez un país con tantos médicos que la junta militar que generosamente había asumido las responsabilidades de gobernar organizó una guerra civil para que se mantuvieran ocupados pero se les olvidó que la falta de tareas los había convertido en una manga de ociosos sin ningún otro interés que el de conseguir prebendas y pagos ilícitos de las compañías químicas y farmacéuticas. Cuando el número de muertos y heridos desatendidos llegó al escándalo el pueblo entero exigió que se pasara por las armas a todos los médicos. Aun cuando hayan pasado ya cinco años de los dramáticos fusilamientos seguimos festejando con abrazos y festivales nuestra gran reconciliación nacional.

# For the Country

Once there was a country with so many doctors that the military junta that had generously taken over the responsibilities of government organized a civil war so the doctors would have plenty of work but they forgot that the earlier lack of cases had turned them into a bunch of lazy bums with no interest beyond getting cushy jobs and taking illegal payoffs from chemical and phamaceutical companies. When the number of neglected dead and wounded became a scandal the entire country demanded that all the doctors be killed. Still five years after the dramatic executions, we keep celebrating our great national reconciliation with embraces and festivals.

# los muchachos de antes

tengo un pecado nuevo que quiero estrenar contigo, eso me dijo pobre viejito endeble la cabeza ardiéndole de boleros que no dejan lugar a ninguna duda ese tiene dentadura postiza y le duelen las encías cuando finge pasarse distraídamente la mano por la mejilla

le duelen las encías y quiere algo con vos no seas tan arrogante tan hijoputesca que vos te mojás por cualquiera a esta edad y él necesita musiquitas, necesita adobo, necesita teatro por eso te canta para que lo acompañes

me parece bien pero decíle que no me siga por la calle o que por lo menos me espere un poco más lejos        me molestaría que me vea mi vieja por ahí lo distrae por ahí se reconocen de algún baile de antes y me deja plantada con los buñuelos mi sombrero de picnic y las ganas de que me monte el teatrito

# now those were men

let's get it on baby, *tengo un pecado nuevo que quiero estrenar con-tigo* that's what he said pitiful wreck of a man old loose den-tures          gums hurting as he touched his cheek as though by chance          head seething with boleros

I tell you his gums are giving him hell and all he wants to do is to have something with you          don't be so cold          bitchy          ar-rogant just think at your age you can get turned on in no time but he needs stuff          sweet tunes          spiced-up dreams that's why he asks for your company with a serenade

O. K. it's all right with me but do tell him not to follow me on the street          meet me farther away          I'd hate for my mom to see me          recognize him from some old dance hall and distract him so that maybe he'll leave me waiting picnic basket ready straw hat all dolled up for our outing          eager for his little show

# Hay que saber cortar a tiempo

En ese país hay un hombre que ha terminado de remendar un par de zoquetes sentado en un banquito. Está junto al teléfono porque su novia le ha prometido que hoy irán a pasear juntos por el parque. Al cabo de cinco años le duele la espalda y decide dejar de esperarla. Se retira de la ventana. Al levantarse se le caen el hilo y la aguja y justo en el momento en que tira las medias a la basura entra la novia sin tocar el timbre, le dice me costó tanto tiempo conseguir un taxi, le presenta a sus dos hijos y se enoja con él para siempre. Naturalmente se va ofendida por la barba crecida, su pinta pasada de moda y la falta general de morisquetas en una cara que de todos modos es demasiado pálida para un amante, único papel que le hubiera venido bien ahora que ella está casada con el amable y generoso taxista que finalmente la recogió una tarde ventosa con chaparrones y brusco descenso de la temperatura.

# Got to Know When
# to Call It Quits

In that country a man sitting on a bench has just finished darning a pair of socks. He's next to the telephone because his girlfriend had promised him that today they'd take a walk together through the park. But after five years his back hurts and he decides not to wait any longer. He moves away from the window. As he stands up the needle and thread fall to the floor and the very moment he throws the socks into the trash the girlfriend comes in, without ringing the doorbell, tells him it took so long to get a taxi, introduces him to her two children, and gets angry at him forever. Naturally she was put off by his long beard, old-fashioned look, and general lack of class in a face that anyway is too pale for a lover, the only role that would have suited him now that she was married to the kind and generous taxi driver who finally picked her up one windy afternoon with showers and a sudden drop in temperature.

# El flete está incluído

Tenemos una clara misión a diferencia de ustedes que se roen las uñas sentados frente a cabinas telefónicas para arreglar encuentros invariablemente inútiles. Nos interesa el comercio exterior y pasamos al lado de ustedes sin conmovernos por el monto de los billetes que indudablemente reciben cada día a cambio de dudosas transacciones comerciales. Sabemos que son pobres tipos y nos agrada abotonarnos los trajes oscuros que vestimos para despistarlos. En el fondo los amamos porque no hay otro modo de relacionarnos con nuestro exclusivo producto de exportación. Sólo nos preocupa que un día rechacen los premios y dejen de entrar mansamente en los excelentes containers etiquetados con sus nombres, destinos y precios al contado.

# Shipping Included

We have a clear goal not like all of you who sit biting your nails in front of telephone booths waiting to arrange meetings that never amount to anything. We're interested in foreign trade and pass by you people unmoved by the stack of bills you undoubtedly receive each day in exchange for shady business deals. We know they are losers and we enjoy buttoning the dark suits we wear to fool them. At bottom we love them because there's no other way to have a relationship with our exclusive export product. Our only concern is that one day they'll turn their backs on the rewards and will let themselves go tamely inside the excellent containers labeled with their names, destinations, and cash prices.

# incompatibilidad de caracteres

*para Rubén Darío*

Otra vez había un mandarín que seguía a una lavandera por la calle. Todas las tardes cuando ella venía de trabajar en casas donde se atascaban los lavarropas o con dueños fóbicos que no querían usar electricidad él la seguía a pie y en palanquín. La lavandera se moría de ganas de darse vuelta y acariciarle la barbita tan puntiaguda, lacia y negra pero tenía miedo de que le pidiera que le lavara el kimono y la seda, ya se sabe, mejor limpiarla a seco.

# irreconcilable differences

*for Rubén Darío*

Another time there was a mandarin who followed a washerwoman in the street. Every afternoon he went after her on foot and by rickshaw as she returned from houses owned by phobic people who did not like to use electricity, or responded to urgent calls from upset customers with malfunctioning washing machines who suddenly discovered her low fees and cleaner habits. The washerwoman was dying to turn around and caress his pointy, straight, and shiny black goatee but she was afraid he would ask her to wash his kimono and as we all know silk must be dry-cleaned.

# Me da una lástima, fíjese

Es una vampira de uñas largas, mamá de un amigo que vive lejos. De vez en cuando recibo cartas enternecedoras pero yo no se las contesto porque no quiero comprometerme. Me estoy reservando para cuando te decidas a confesarme tus sentimientos.

# How not pity him?

She's a long-nailed vampire, the mother of a distant friend. From time to time I receive her moving letters but I do not reply because I do not want to get into a compromising situation. I am saving myself for you, darling. Any day now you'll tell me what you've been hiding.

# Igual que en el cine

Las chicas que miran televisión creen que al apagarla comienza su vida. POBRECITAS. No se dan cuenta de que el tubo les ha absorbido el mate y ahora, poquito a poco, les viene la felicidad a intervalos precisos, como la menstruación o los avisos publicitarios.

# Just Like a Movie

The girls watching TV believe that their lives start when they they turn it off. POOR THINGS. They don't realize that the set has sucked their minds dry and now, little by little, happiness comes to them periodically, like menstruation or television ads.

# Hay que compartir
# las oportunidades

En esta ciudad las viejas se visten de adolescentes y las jóvenes de viejas porque así cada una consigue el trabajo de la otra.

# Let's Not Be Selfish

In this town old women dress as teenagers and the young as old because that way each is available to do the job of the other.

# una mujer debe saber vestirse para la ocasión

La princesita bizca me mira con ojos entornados porque le da vergüenza que me entere que no le han dejado que se opere de la vista. Sabe que de todos modos jugaremos a las cartas todo el tiempo que quiera. Yo la dejo ganar. Igual me da lo mismo       para qué quiero ahora todas esas joyas que perdí hace años       de qué me servirían los palacios o los arrumacos de mi príncipe así       a la intemperie y sin nada que ponerme.

# a woman must know how to dress for the part

The cute, cross-eyed young princess looks at me with downcast eyes because she is embarrassed because she was denied permission to have eye surgery. She knows that I'll play cards with her anyway for as long as she wants. I let her win. I don't give a damn. Why do I need all the jewelry I lost to her years ago now          what purpose would I have in owning palaces or having my prince's amorous attentions since I am homeless and have nothing to wear?

# Renovarse es vivir

El pueblo que queda cerca de la ciudad tiene una habitación para las mujeres desesperadas del centro. Allí se apretujan para contarse los agravios recibidos, se ponen delineador de cejas y salen, temibles, panteras, a lo que se ofrezca.

# Time to Move On

In a suburb bordering the city there is a room for downtown women at the end of their rope. They crowd in there to tell their grievances, apply eyeliner, and go out again, fearsome panthers ready for anything.

# ¿Qué querés? Todos tenemos derecho a la felicidad

En este país todos duermen y todos cantan cuando se despiertan porque la reina los ama, les da regalos y les pone compresas para los escalofríos. Si desean mejorarse es porque su mayor esperanza reside en querer envejecer a su lado. Conductora. Corderitos. Orgía de mimos y festivales gratuitos. Me parece que ella nunca supo nunca se dio cuenta de cómo se deshacían de los intrusos     cómo defendían las fronteras     conservaban la intimidad y el amor que los une.

# What Do You Think? Everybody Has a Right to Be Happy

Here people sleep and sing first thing in the morning thanks to the queen's devotion, she bestows gifts and even applies warm compresses when they have a chill. They strive to do better because their main wish is to get old with her at their side. She will be their leader forever, acquiescent lambs in an orgy of pampering and giveaways. I believe that she never knew never realized how they got rid of intruders        how they guarded their borders to preserve the intimacy and the love that binds them.

# La mujer invisible /
# The Invisible Woman

# ¿No te enteraste?

Ese día todos celebraban que el país se había trasladado a un hemisferio más frío. De ese modo no tardarían tanto en llegar las liquidaciones de invierno y podrían lucir esos abrigos de piel que siempre quedan bien para las funciones de gala. Pobrecitos, frívolos, distraídos, pasatistas. Se perdieron el nacimiento casi sin gemidos de una criatura con vocación de rincones y andar silencioso. Fue un acontecimiento casero sin rasgos distintivos. No hubo fiesta. Nadie se acuerda de cómo la llamaron porque ella es la invisible. Personalmente te confieso que no le tengo envidia y eso, en mi caso que, como sabes, es muy particular, es mucho decir.

# Didn't You Notice?

That day everyone was celebrating because the country had moved to a colder hemisphere. That way the winter sales would come much sooner and they could show off those fur coats that go so well with gala events. Poor things, frivolous, distracted, out of it. They missed the birth almost without a moan of an infant girl with a liking for corners and silent step. It was a household event with nothing special about it. There was no party. Nobody remembered her name because she was invisible. Personally I confess to you that I do not envy her and, for me, as you know, that is very special, that's saying a lot.

# Dieta

La mujer invisible se atraganta con ciruelas, uvas, cualquier cosa redonda y sufre náuseas con las insaladas, especialmente los blinis con caviar rosado que se sirven en la embajada de la República Checa cuando llegan dignatarios de países desarrollados en los cuales la gente juega al tenis y usa zapatillas que suspiran como si fueran alfombras en la cámara nupcial de un palacio vuelto hotel después de la ya superada revolución pero naturalmente ella no lo sabe porque no ha tenido ni tendrá oportunidad de probar esos manjares. Juraría que no va a ningún lado, aunque por ahí pasó y no la reconozco.

# Diet

The invisible woman chokes on cherries, grapes, anything round, and is made nauseous by salads, especially blinis with red caviar that they serve in the embassy of the Czech Republic when dignitaries arrive from developed countries where people play tennis and wear sneakers that sigh like carpets in the nuptial suite of a palace now hotel after the recent revolution but naturally she didn't know any of this because she's never had the opportunity to try those delicacies. I would swear that she doesn't go anywhere, although she passed by here and I didn't recognize her.

# detrás de cada mujer hay otra

Ella me tiene rencor y a mí no me importa porque su odio me hace engalanarme más. Pienso en ella noche y día, me comparo con sus caderas llovidas, el vestido gris que indudablemente usa para salir de compras. La adoro cuando me despierto con el olor de su carne chamuscada y salgo corriendo, queridos, salgo disparada porque no soporto su peso en mis horas, este agujero, esta payasada de mierda.

# behind every woman
## there is another

She resents me but I don't care because her hatred makes me try and doll myself up even more. I think about her night and day, measure myself against her droopy hips. I see her clearly: sagging breasts in the gray dress she undoubtedly wears to go grocery shopping. I adore her when I wake up, the stench of her burning flesh still in my nostrils and I rush out, my friends, I run away because I can't stand the burden of her existence weighing on me every hour, this hole, this fucking charade.

# amores que matan

Había una vez un leñador que le daba leña todos los días a una morocha que le decía más más que si no me das se me corta el apetito me seco toda la vida no tiene sentido dame más fuerte por favor.

# love that kills

Once upon a time there was a whip-maker who whipped a dark-haired woman every night while she begged him    more more give me more if you don't let me have it good and hard    I'll dry out    lose my appetite    life will have no meaning give it to me harder please.

# no me des vuelta la cara

La próxima vez me tomo un taxi.
La próxima vez me compro zapatos cómodos.
La próxima vez le pego una bofetada.
La próxima vez en lugar de escaparme me quedo y le canto cuatro verdades con voz de cigarrillo.
La próxima vez desnuda frente a la ventana le armo un escándalo le digo mira mi sangre come mis pestañas necesito desodorante.

# don't give me the cold shoulder

Next time I'll take a cab.
Next time I'll buy comfortable shoes.
Next time I'll slap him.
Next time instead of running away I'll stay and tell him what's what
in a hoarse cigarette voice.
Next time naked facing the window I'll raise hell     tell him look at
my blood eat my eyelashes run get me deodorant.

# Basta la salud

Tiene un ataque al hígado. De eso se dan cuenta. Ellos son toda dulzura y la untan con mantequilla pero como su carne no es lo suficientemente jugosa para el sandwich, estómagos trinando se van corriendo al restaurante de la esquina mientras a ella se le apagan otra vez las luces y, doblada, espasmódica, pega grititos, aullidos y le hace caritas al canario que se retuerce en la jaula como si le pasara algo.

# Health Is Everything

She has a splitting headache. They realized what it was. They are all sweetness and smear her with butter but since her flesh is not juicy enough for a sandwich, stomachs growling they go running to the restaurant on the corner and as for her they turn off the lights again and, bent double, in spasms, she shouts, howls, and makes faces at the canary that twists around in its cage as if something were wrong with it.

# ¿Alguien vió de dónde vino el disparo?

Tesoro:

Cuando te fuiste me sentí abandonada. Quise hacerte recordar mi nombre y apellido en el día de nuestro aniversario y me dolió que me devolvieran las cartas. Por eso te pido disculpas y te dedico este último gesto para que un día de estos alguien coloque nuestros nombres juntos por los siglos de los siglos.

# Anyone See Where the Shot Came From?

Dearest treasure:

I felt so lost when you up and left me. All I wanted was to help you remember my full name on our anniversary, and that's why I felt hurt when my letters were returned. I beg your forgiveness and dedicate this last gesture to you so that one of these days somebody may inscribe our names together forever and ever.

# ¿Adónde vas este año?

En verano se llama Patricia y nunca va a la playa. Está en la ciudad. Camina por las calles del centro con una cartera negra de la cual saca un Kleenex porque está resfriada o acaso tenga alergia. Poco importa. A nosotros nos gustan las chicas en malla, los muchachos que se ponen bronceador en los músculos para que les brillen y las mamás jóvenes que aún huelen a semen y leche. Nos gustan en serio. Qué nos vamos a preocupar por ella. Qué sabe de vacaciones. Qué mosca le habrá picado. Por qué no se pone al día, mira televisión, pega un gritito.

# Where Are You Going This Year?

In summer she's called Patricia and never goes to the beach. She's in the city. She walks through the downtown streets carrying a black purse from which she takes a Kleenex because she has a cold or maybe allergies. It doesn't matter. As for us we like to see girls in bathing suits, boys who oil their muscles so they gleam, and young mothers still smelling of semen and milk. We really do like them. Why should we worry about her? What does she know about vacations? What's the matter with her anyway? Why doesn't she get with the times, watch television, let out a little cry?

# Hay algunas que te parten el alma

Le tiene envidia hasta a las moscas. Asco, lo que se dice asco, no le tiene a nada. Sabe que un día tranquilo la llevarán en andas. Caminarán rápido casi sin darse cuenta de que está ahí. Pobrecita. Tan embadurnada de sus agravios que casi sonríe, casi nos pide que le celebremos el cumpleaños.

# They'll Break Your Heart

She is even jealous of flies. Nothing will make her puke. She knows that one calm day they'll take her up on their shoulders and off they'll go, so fast they'll even forget that she's there. Poor baby, so besmirched by their insults yet almost smiles, almost asks us to celebrate her birthday.

# Me gusta como personaje

Había una vez una princesa muy pobre que contaba sus centavos sentada en el alfeizar de una ventana. Le faltaban:

1. el coraje de salir a buscar trabajo en las tiendas del centro
2. la autorización de los ministros para pedir limosna en nombre de la nación
3. el vistobueno de la iglesia que disolvería su matrimonio
4. un par de jeans para sustituir este vestido que me queda tan ajustado y que de raído parece un trapo de piso y no la ropa de gala que los ayudará a soñarme bailando en los brazos de un novio sin pancita ni olor a grasa.

# What a Character

Once upon a time there was a very poor princess who was counting her coins while sitting in the embrasure of a window. She was missing:

1. the courage to go out and look for work in the downtown stores
2. the permission of the ministers to be allowed to beg for charity in the name of the nation
3. the approval of the church for the annulment of her marriage
4. a pair of jeans to replace her dress that is too tight and so worn it looks like a rag to clean the floor and not the kind of party dress that would make you dream of me dancing in the arms of a slender, sweet-smelling suitor.

# Nena, me muero por vos

Cuando se encuentran ella le da un pellizco detrás de la oreja derecha y él suspira emocionado porque desde hace rato tratan de co-
nocerse pero no sé por qué les sobreviene una vergüenza terrible y
se separan hasta el día siguiente. Ella se llama Nancy. Le han crecido
las uñas desde la primera cita pero como él realmente la quiere con
locura no se queja de las gotitas de sangre que le arranca ni aún
mañana ni pasado ni más adelante cuando le salga a borbotones.

# Help, Baby, I'm Dying For You

When they meet she pinches him behind the right ear and he sighs, moved because they have been trying to get closer for a while but for some reason they are embarrassed and part until the next day. Her name is Nancy. Her nails have grown since their first date but since he loves her madly he does not utter a complaint about the blood-drops when she pinches him not even tomorrow or after tomorrow or later on when it will start flowing like a river.

# Te guardo en el alma

De todos sus amores el suyo fue el único que la dejó intacta.

# From the Heart

Of all her loves his was the only one that left her whole.

# Cómo no te vas a acordar de mí si de chicos éramos inseparables, che

Sarita, Ana y Nicolás espían a Francisco, Alejandro y María. Francisco se va al extranjero y se vuelve tan famoso que Alejandro y María les pagan todo lo que tienen a Sarita, Ana y Nicolás para que les revelen sus secretos. Así se dan cuenta de que Francisco ha estado enamorado de María desde que eran niños y que, seguro de que Alejandro se casaría con ella, partió, amasó riqueza y decidió no regresar al lugar de su derrota. Naturalmente Sarita, Ana, Nicolás, Alejandro y María consiguen pasajes gratuitos a Suiza en un avión de la fuerza aérea con la promesa de compartir el dinero que Francisco les dará para que no le cuenten a su mujer que María está ahora dispuesta a abandonar a Alejandro por él y vivir la gran pasión de su vida. Llegan a Suiza con una delegación de niños cantores que les pisan los zapatos de suela de goma y, medio mareados por la falta de costumbre y el cambio de continente, pierden la cara de la adolescencia, la viveza de barrio. Cuando finalmente Francisco los atiende en su oficina, apenas los reconoce. Pero es tan amable, tan elegante y tan generoso que antes de irse le pide a su secretaria que les sirva té con masitas previo llamado a la policía desde un botoncito especialmente instalado en la solapa, debajo de las condecoraciones internacionales. Fascinerosos. Muertos de hambre. A esos se los conoce de lejos. Son iguales en todos lados.

# How Can You Not Remember Me If As Kids Nobody Could Pull Us Apart?

Sarita, Ana, and Nicolás are spying on Francisco, Alejandro, and María. Francisco goes abroad and becomes so famous that Alejandro and María give everything they have to Sarita, Ana, and Nicolás so they'll tell them their secrets. That's how they know that Francisco has been in love with María ever since they were children and sure that Alejandro will marry her, Francisco left, got rich, and decided not to return to the place of his defeat. Naturally Sarita, Ana, Nicolás, Alejandro, and María get free tickets to Switzerland in an air force plane with the promise of sharing the money that Francisco will give them so they won't tell his wife that María is now ready to leave Alejandro for him and to live the grand passion of her life. They arrive in Switzerland with a delegation of child singers wearing rubber-soled shoes and, made half-dizzy by the different customs and the change of continent, lose their adolescent look, the liveliness of the old neighborhood. When Francisco finally receives them in his office, he hardly recognizes them. But he is so amiable, so elegant, and so generous that before leaving he asks his secretary to serve them tea with cookies even though he has already called the police from a little button installed in his lapel, beneath the international decorations. Crooks. Bums. You can recognize them a mile away. They're the same everywhere.

# Hacéme caso, el amor no es ciego

El alcalde vive solo porque quiere. Detrás de su puerta se debaten las muertas de hambre. Estúpidas. Creen que les dará todo por su nada. Sabemos que dentro de treinta y cinco días su asistente, cansado de tanto olor a mujerona en celo, les repartirá estas escarapelas tan patrióticas, tan de época.

# Believe Me, Love's Not Blind

The ruler lives alone because he wants to. Behind his door a crowd of starving women talk among themselves. Fools. They think he'll give them everything for nothing. We know that in thirty-five days his assistant, tired of the thick smell of women in heat, will distribute these insignias so patriotic, so traditional and becoming.

# A caballo regalado

La mujer invisible me ha comprado un regalo. Me lo llevo a la cama, lo acaricio y pienso en la otra, la chica medio bizca de la peluquería. Pienso en la otra y me siento hermosa sin su pelo grasiento ni las uñas con esmalte saltado. La mujer invisible tiene una cartera de doble fondo para el cuchillito que nos ofrecerá después del festín.

# Let's Not Be Choosy Now

The invisible woman has bought me a gift. I take it to bed with me, caress it, and think about the other one, the cross-eyed girl at the hairdresser's. I think about her and feel beautiful without her oily hair and nails with chipped polish. The invisible woman has a pocketbook with a false bottom for concealing the dainty knife she will offer us after the banquet.

# ¡Primicia!

JUAN: Devolvéme la pelota.

PEDRO: Vení a buscarla, no seas cobarde.

JUAN: Devolvéme la medallita.

PEDRO: Vení a buscarla, no seas pelotudo.

JUAN: Devolvéme a mi novia.

PEDRO: Esa mina no valía nada. La despaché hace rato.

JUAN: Devolvéme el diario.

PEDRO: Tomá. Leélo. Igual, nuestra noticia no sale hasta mañana, cuando nos encuentren.

# Scoop!

JUAN: Give me back the ball.
PEDRO: Come get it, don't be chicken.
JUAN: Give me back the medal.
PEDRO Come get it, don't be a jerk.
JUAN: Give me back my girl.
PEDRO That chick was worth nothing. I got rid of her some time ago.
JUAN: Give me back the newspaper.
PEDRO: Here. Read it. All the same, our news doesn't come out until
  tomorrow, when we run into one another.

# hay que saber dar vuelta la tortilla

Cuando los peregrinos llegaron al pueblo fueron muy bien recibidos por los nativos que hablaban idiomas muy importantes:

inglés
francés
alemán

conocían las leyes del mercado y los numerosos beneficios del turismo y debido a eso estaban preparadísimos para la visita     les distribuyeron comida, unas chozas al borde del río e inmediatamente los pusieron a trabajar de nativos para los turistas, que deleitados ante tanto color local alegraban los cocktail parties de las embajadas y gastaban sus exóticas divisas en souvenirs y manjares para alardear delante de amigos y familiares que emprenderían idénticos itinerarios con cámaras de video y oídos sordos de tanta música folklórica.

# got to move with the times

When the pilgrims arrived in town they were very well received by the natives who spoke major languages:

English
French
German

they knew about the laws of the market and the many benefits afforded by tourism    that's why they were ready for the visit and had enough food to go around    cabanas with a river view, and jobs for them to perform the role of natives for tourists, who delighted at the display of local color and enlivened cocktail party after cocktail party at embassies and hotels freely spending their exotic currency on souvenirs and new foods so that family and friends would admire them and plan identical itineraries complete with video cameras and ears already deafened by too much folk music.

# Sin comentarios

Si recorre sus tierras le viene un vacío en el estómago y sale corriendo a vomitar. Prefiere tomar fotos desde el balcón. Aunque me molestan sus coqueteos, poso con todos mis amigos y espero atentamente mi turno.

# Beyond Words

If he surveys his land he is overcome by an emptiness in the pit of his stomach that makes him rush out to throw up. He prefers to take pictures from the balcony. Although I am put off by his insinuations, I pose with all my friends and politely await my turn.

# que la dejen sola solita y sola que la quiero ver bailar

Compra
   vestidos
      collares
         un camisón de tela áspera y botas de cuero para hacer
         juego con su latiguito

amor mío te ruego que no la persigas          hay que dejarla donde
esté        no entrar en el juego

# don't move! watch how she goes at it by herself

She buys
    dresses
        necklaces
            a prickly nightgown and leather boots to match her little
            whip

please my sweetheart I beg you don't run after her        she's got to
be left just where she is        let's not get sucked into her game

# Yo que vos, me quedo en casa

La tía de la condesa vive lejísimo pero de todos modos la han llamado para que asista a la intervención quirúrgica. El resto de la familia la considera una intrusa. Plebeya. Desarreglada. Ofendidísimos, le envenenan el calmante y tratan de convencer a la tía de que se quede a cenar con ellos. Figuráte, por qué no relajarse después de semejante viaje.

# In Your Place, I'd Stay Home

The aunt of the countess lives way out in the boonies but in any case they've called her so she can be present during the surgery. The rest of the family considers her an interloper. Common. Sloppy. Highly offended, they poison the sedative and try to convince the aunt to stay and have supper with them. After all, why not relax after such a trek?

# no, yo pensaba nada más

Si la mujer invisible usara vestidos transparentes todos los poetas y los rockeros adolescentes se enamorarían de ella pero no te preocupes porque no tiene sentido de la moda y es incapaz de robarte mi admiración, este suspiro.

# just a passing thought

If the invisible woman wore see-through dresses every poet and teenage rock fan would fall in love with her but don't worry because she doesn't have the slightest fashion sense and is completely incapable of making me stop sighing with admiration for you.

# Rincón de los profetas / Prophet's Corner

# ¿me interpreta?

Los profetas están reunidos para coleccionar las palabras del futuro. Cada uno elige la del otro, la pule, conjuga y trata de apropiársela para siempre. Pero como se trata de palabras caprichosas, enamoradas de sus antiguos dueños, ellas se retraen, evocan los bolsillos de antes y en el afán de volver no se dan cuenta de que ya están ahí.

# you get it?

The prophets are holding a meeting to collect words for the future. Each chooses one from the other, polishes it, conjugates it and tries to steal it forever. But since these are whimsical words, enamored of their previous owners, they hold back, remember their past places, and in the midst of their haste to return they don't even realize that they have already arrived.

# el profeta en su propia tierra

ay, si te contara
ay si pudieras verme
ay si de repente       toda vestida de negro       y una pluma en
la cabeza salieras a anunciar nuestro escándalo y bailaras la conga
acompañada de las tres chicas que hoy me negarán el saludo

# the prophet in his own land

oh, if you only knew
oh, if you could see me now
oh, if all of a sudden clad in black     feathers on your head you
would come to blurt out our secret     lead a conga line with the
same three girls who will shun me today

# coqueterías de profeta lector

Con chinelas nuevas y un pijama a cuadros ha llegado a la biblioteca. No quieren prestarle libros. Se acuerdan de que la última vez borroneó todas las fechas. Es lógico. Para él todo es cuestión de tiempo excepto su calvicie.

# quirks of a reader prophet

He arrives in the library sporting new slippers and plaid pajamas. They refuse to let him borrow books. They remember how he changed all the due dates last time. It figures. For him everything is a matter of time except for his baldness.

# el profeta viaja en el Titanic

Miraba a la rubia con el sentido preciso de su valor. Miraba a la rubia y pensaba en cómo luciría la tarde en que aferrados a la balsa comprendieran que nadie llegaría a salvarlos. Miraba a la rubia y aún así no se atrevía a hablarle. Vergüenza de estar en el centro de la ciudad, pisar tierra firme. Creo que por eso anhelaba tanto el naufragio, los estertores del espanto, la vuelta final.

# the prophet travels on the Titanic

He watched the blonde appraising her precise value. He watched the blonde and thought of the moment when, holding on to the raft, they would realize that nobody would come to save them. He watched the blonde and still couldn't bring himself to talk to her. What a shame to be downtown stepping on firm ground. I know that's why he so wished to be shipwrecked, be terrified, take a perilous turn.

# lucha de clases I

Los profetas tienen sus flores predilectas pero no se lo dicen a nadie porque son concientes de que desaparecerían inmediatamente del borde del camino. No osan mirarlas ni mucho menos cortarlas. La gente es egoísta. Mejor ocultarse en un rincón y oler extracto de unas botellitas diminutas fabricadas en países del futuro por chicos que ya no necesitan ir a la escuela. Mejor esperar dicen estos profetas de barrio y se pelean hasta el cansancio con los profetas del centro que quieren abrir florerías, kioskos, agencias de inmuebles.

# class struggle I

Prophets have favorite flowers but they don't let anyone know which ones they are because they know that as soon as the news got out the plants would be uprooted. They don't even dare look at much less touch them. People are selfish. Better to hide in a corner and inhale their fragrance from minute bottles produced in future-minded countries by kids who are no longer required to attend school. Better to wait, advise those suburban prophets, and fight tirelessly against downtown prophets who want to open flower shops, news-stands, and real estate agencies.

# lucha de clases 3

Revuelo de profetas uniformados que meten a profetas armados e inocentes como capullitos en cárceles vigiladas por gente con sentido mercantil. Gritos, gritos y aullidos de fuentes periodísticas y universitarias. Gran silencio de los vecinos que, resfriados, deciden tomar más y más té, vino y agua mineral. Total, como dicen todos los profetas, esto no puede seguir así.

# class struggle 3

Uproar of uniformed prophets who put armed and innocent prophets like so many greenhorn recruits into prisons guarded by business types. Screams, cries, and yelps from media and academic sources. Great silence on the part of the neighbors, all loudmouths, who decide to drink more and more tea, wine, and mineral water. The upshot, as all prophets say, is that things can't go on this way.

# profeta enamorado de mujer sin visión del futuro

desvaría por generosidad
cuando abre los ojos se los restriega para no ver
tiene problemas con una novia que le exige más y más confidencias
y él le dice dejáte de embromar dame otra masita traéme una
empanada
este beso me gustó más que el de hace un rato y menos que el de
ahora

# prophet smitten by a woman with no sense of the future

he daydreams out of generosity
when he comes out of it he rubs his eyes until he can't see
he's got problems with a girlfriend who demands more and more intimate chitchat
and he tells her don't bother me give me another cookie bring me an empanada
I liked this kiss better than the last one and less than the one you are giving me now

# adorno para recién casados

*los profetas nunca se equivocan cuando mienten*

# house gift for newlyweds

*prophets are never wrong when they are lying*

# dejá, se arreglan solas

Había una vez una pacífica colonia de hormiguitas que dió a luz a un profeta. Se dieron cuenta enseguida por su desidia, la manera en que usaba las hojas como colchón en vez de transportarlas disciplinadamente en fila india. No hizo siquiera falta que lo vieran panza arriba hablándole íntimamente a una mariposa. Suerte. Porque así     mientras él se ocupaba de la gran transición histórica lo pusieron en la línea de ataque del insecticida. Después se marcharon como nos gusta     una detrás de la otra y fueron felices y comieron perdices.

# give it up, they'll manage
# by themselves

Once there was a peaceful colony of ants that gave birth to a prophet. They knew it right away because he was so lazy and because he used the leaves as a mattress instead of carrying them Indian file in regimented order. It was even quite common to see him lying belly-up having a heart-to-heart conversation with a butterfly. Lucky. Because that way while he was dealing with the great historical transition they put him in the front line of the insecticide. Later they kept on marching one after the other the way we like them to do and felt dandy and ate candy.

# después de la revolución

Otra vez los esclavos jugaban a las figuritas. Entonces llegó la diva con un muchachito muy delgado que se escurrió ante el primer silbido de admiración. No se preocupen, sigan jugando, sigan nomás tesoritos les dijo la diva y ellos pendientes de su encanto ni se dieron cuenta cuando el flaquito regresó a lustrarles la cadena con la cera que compramos a precios internacionales en el duty free.

# after the revolution

Once again the slaves were swapping baseball cards. Then the diva arrived with an emaciated young man who slipped away at the first wolf whistle. Don't worry, go on with your game, keep it up, sweethearts, the diva ordered them and they were so taken with her many charms that they didn't even notice when the skinny kid came back to polish their chain with the wonderful wax we get at international rates in duty-free shops.

# ¡Sonreí! Te estamos autobiografiando / Smile! We Are Autobiographing You

# la criamos como si fuera nuestra

Nací de chiquita en una casa donde había mucha gente mayor que hablaba entre sí de una pelea que habían tenido hacía algunos años a raíz de la distribución de una herencia robada por una persona embarazada que había huído raudamente después de dar a luz a una criatura que pobrecita no tenía la culpa de nada. Nací aliviada de tanto escucharlos y por eso digo que no          me escapo          no hago los deberes y les saco la lengua cada vez que me piden que les lave los calzoncillos y prepare el desayuno para sus hijos.

# we raised her as if she were our own

I was born when I was a little girl in a house full of older people who talked among themselves about a fight they'd had some years earlier because of the distribution of an inheritance stolen by a pregnant woman who'd fled in a great rush after giving birth to a baby girl who poor thing was guilty of nothing. From birth I knew I was innocent just from listening to them talk and that's why I say no          I run away          skip my homework          stick out my tongue at them each time they want to boss me around          wash their underpants          make breakfast for their children.

## que me tomen por otra

Me llamo Norma pero no se lo digo a nadie. En vez, me presento como Carmen y los oigo dale que dale con el amor y las castañuelas. El que más me pudre es mi marido por más que me duerma antes de que se acueste       le mande anónimos       y le deje comida fría e indigesta sigue diciéndome que siempre pero siempre tenía la ilusión de casarse con una carmen como la virgen.

# let them take me
# for someone else

My name is Norma but I won't tell anyone. I introduce myself as Carmen instead and let them go on and on about love and cymbals. The one who gets to me the worst is my husband even if I fall sleep before he comes to bed, send him anonymous messages, and leave him cold, heavy-as-a-rock meals while he keeps on telling me that he always hoped to marry a carmen just like the virgin.

# ¿Y esto te parece vida?

Empecé a escribir la historia de mi vida un día en que no pasaba nada y me vinieron a la cabeza tantas verdades que desde entonces encerrada en mi pieza con las cortinas bajas lleno cuaderno tras cuaderno y les digo déjenme tranquila       no no quiero de las de queso       tráiganme de mermelada y por favor cambien la botella de leche que creo que es la misma desde hace por los menos dos años.

# You Call This a Life?

I began to write the story of my life one day when nothing was happening and so many truths came into my head that ever since closed up in my room with the curtains drawn I fill notebook after notebook and I say to them leave me alone I don't want cheese bring me marmalade and please change the bottle of milk that I think is the same one that's been here for at least the past two years.

# mis gustos

Siempre me gustó la gente. Cuando tenía diez años me fui a trabajar en un circo y si no hubiera sido por el olor a elefante que me penetraba hasta las encías y le daba sabor a los alfajores que el domador de leones me cocinaba por las tardes, todavía estaría ahí.

Si fuera verdaderamente callejera no estaría contándote estas cosas pero te confieso que cuando llueve salgo con el expreso deseo de encontrarte en un café refugiándote como yo de tanto viento y humedad.

Uno más y me voy pero qué le voy a hacer tomo otro y otro y después juego a no contarlos.

# things I like

I've always liked people. When I was ten years old I went to work in a circus and I'd still be there if it hadn't been for the elephant smell that permeated the gums and left the taste of the pastries the lion tamer made for me in the evenings.

If I were really streetwise I wouldn't be telling you these things but I confess to you that when it rains I go out on purpose to find you hiding out in a café like me to get out of so much wind and dampness.

One more and I'll go but what does it matter to you if I have another and another and afterwards pretend not to count them.

# hay cosas que te atan

Pensé irme ni bien llegué pero la comitiva fue tan persuasiva que me quedé con ellos a contar papas fritas en el restaurante. Había que hacer un inventario muy detallado, acostarse con los clientes para que no escribieran evaluaciones negativas, coimear al inspector y congraciarse con el dueño de modo de que no nos echara. Entretanto, las papas fritas cada vez más grasosas aprendieron a hablar y nos cantaban composiciones folklóricas de países del tercer mundo. Evidentemente no puedo irme ahora que estoy tan compenetrada de todo esto. ¿Cómo dejarlo por una libretita de direcciones y el recuerdo de mis cumpleaños?

# setting down roots

The minute I arrived I thought I'd leave but the group was so persuasive that I stayed with them to count french fries in the restaurant. We were expected to make a very detailed inventory, sleep with the customers so they wouldn't write negative evaluations, bribe the inspector, ingratiate ourselves with the boss so he wouldn't throw us out. In the meantime the fries greasier and greasier learned to talk and sing folk songs from third-world countries to us. Obviously I can't go now that I am up to my neck in all this. How could I leave it for a little address book and the souvenir of my birthday?

# vida de hogar

Era un matrimonio muy correcto que decidió dar a luz a huérfanos. Les agradaba la formalidad, la conducta silenciosa y respetuosa de esos niños que se encuentran en orfelinatos y casas de caridad. Los vecinos alababan la educación que brindaban a sus hijos y ellos, orgullosos, siguieron negándoles el uso de la palabra y llevándolos a fiestas familiares hasta la mayoría de edad.

# home sweet home

Once upon a time there was a very respectable couple who decided to give birth to orphans. They loved the formality, and the silent and respectful behavior typical of children in state institutions. All the neighbors praised how well they raised their kids, and the couple, proud, kept encouraging them to keep quiet and accompany them to every family occasion until age twenty-one.

# estaba de novela

Nunca les cuento nada a mis amigas porque son unas estúpidas y me miran embobadas. A quien le insisto con mis secretos es al profesor de historia. Es un pelirrojo que usa Old Spice y calcetines a cuadros. Hace como que me escucha pero sé que en el fondo sólo huele mis ganas y se pone más y más colonia para regarlas todos los días de diez a diez cuarenta y cinco entre las guerras de la independencia y la organización nacional.

# what a hunk

I never tell anything to my girlfriends they're so stupid and look at me mouths hanging open. The one I persist in telling my secrets to is the history professor. He's a redhead who uses Old Spice and wears argyle socks. He pretends he's listening to me but I know that deep down he's only smelling my desires and putting on more and more cologne to feed the flame every day from ten to ten forty-five between the wars of independence and the time of national reorganization.

# en casa de herrero, cuchillo de palo

Hoy hice las valijas porque me voy de viaje a una playa carísima donde trabajo de adivina. Me dan unos desayunos magníficos y se sacan fotos conmigo antes y después del horóscopo. Como se imaginan ruego día y noche para que me renueven el contrato pero con los tiempos que corren quién sabe qué los divertirá el año que viene.

# que será, será

All packed. Today I am going off to a very expensive beach resort where I work as a fortune-teller. They give me these great breakfasts and have their pictures taken with me before and after I do their horoscopes. As you may imagine, I pray night and day that they'll renew my contract but these days who knows what will amuse them next year.

# movie fan

He sido muy feliz entre sus brazos, sobre todo cuando pensaba en todas las películas que veríamos juntos.

# movie fan

I've been very happy in his arms, above all when I thought of all the movies we would watch together.

# nos debemos al público

Los vecinos chismean día y noche sobre mí. Los espío. Intercepto sus teléfonos. Escucho sus conversaciones por las rendijas. Con unos o dos cómplices salgo a hacer complicados paseos para que me sigan hasta entrada la noche y regresen después a compartir indicios, sugerencias, hipótesis. Mi vida es un conjunto de pistas. Se las regalo para que me las devuelvan a escondidas y cuchicheando.

# we owe ourselves to the public

The neighbors gossip about me day and night. I spy on them. Tap their telephones. Listen to their conversations through the cracks. With one or two accomplices I go out walking take complicated routes so they'll follow me until after dark and will then come back to compare signs, suggestions, hypotheses. My life is a collection of clues that I offer them to be returned to me in secret and in whispers.

# a mí no me gusta la violencia

En esta foto la vemos muy erguida. No por orgullo. Le duele un pie. Si miramos con atención notaremos que el caballo que la ha traído hasta aquí yace desvanecido, todo el peso sobre el dedo grande de su pie derecho. Particularmente notable es la mala calidad de sus botas que parecen no haber resistido la humedad del bosque ni la insistencia del estiércol en las suelas. Yo debo evitar mirarla de frente porque de solo pensar en los mosquitos me pica la nariz.

# me, I don't like violence

In this photo we see her standing very erect. Not out of pride. Her foot hurts. If we look closely we will see that the horse that has brought her here lies in a dead faint, all his weight resting on the big toe of her right foot. Particularly noticeable is the poor quality of her boots that seem not to have resisted the dampness of the forest nor the constant manure on the soles. I shouldn't look straight at her because the very thought of the mosquitoes makes my nose itch.

# se busca señorita
# de buena presencia

Ay qué prudente que es
            siempre con la hermanita menor
    Ay qué sana
        qué limpia
            qué tímida
*compra su ropa interior en tiendas de segunda mano*
*la hemos visto la vemos mejillas encendidas ojos entrecerrados busca que*
*te busca*
*los estertores de la primera dueña las huellas del otro del desconocido que*
*la azotará hasta que sin aliento abandone a la hermanita en una plaza*
*y huya para siempre a dormitorios con olor a talco        agua de colo-*
*nia y sábanas manchadas*

# wanted: attractive young woman

Oh how prudent she is
        always with her younger sister
  Oh how healthy
     how neat
       how timid
*she buys her underwear in second-hand stores*
*we've seen her cheeks burning and eyes half-closed hunting and hunting*
*the death rattles of the first boss the tracks of the other the stranger that*
*will beat her until breathless she abandons the little sister in a square*
*and flees forever to bedrooms smelling of talcum powder cologne and*
*stained sheets*

# Locas / Fruitcakes

# de atar

A esta le sobró la mano fuerte y se desquita con una nena juiciosa que pide permiso para ir al cine. Se llama Manuelita. Usa una blusita de encaje los días feriados. El guardapolvo le queda planchado con solo ponérselo. Menos que nena parece una estaca. Todo hasta que llega al sótano de su pecado y con las otras baila que te baila olvidado de su teatro Manuelita la del aliento caliente y los calzoncillos de seda natural fabricados en Hong Kong.

# fit to be tied

They let her have it too hard and now she gets back at a nerdy little girl who asks her permission to go to the movies. Manuelita they call her. Wears a lacy camisole on holidays and for school a uniform that looks ironed as soon as she puts it on her stiff body. Looks more like a stick than a girl. That is, until he gets to her own sinful bottom and dances on forgetting his playacting Manuelita of the hot breath and silk underwear imported directly from Hong Kong.

# con plata es otra cosa

Había una vez tres mujeres que salieron a comprarse sobrinos. La feria estaba atestada de jóvenes postulantes con caras obsecuentes y uñas limpias pero ellas naturalmente busca que te busca encontraron tres con olor a sarro y zapatos demasiado brillosos. Hasta el día de hoy las cosas andan fenómeno porque a ellas les interesa sobre todo que les hagan masajes y les traigan noticias de la familia pero me palpito que cuando vean lo que Roque les trajo de regalo saldrán corriendo a reclamar que les devuelvan sus ahorros        que les saquen de encima a estos cochinos        vividores        jóvenes sin respeto ni sentido de la ocasión.

# what you could do with money

Once there were three women who went out to buy themselves some nephews. The fair was jammed with young prospects with obsequious faces and clean nails but of course the women kept looking and looking until they found three smelling of tartar and wearing unbearably shiny shoes. Until today everything went splendidly because what the women wanted most was for the boys to give them massages and bring them news of the family but I have a hunch that when the ladies see what Roque brought them as a present they'll run out into the streets shouting that their savings be returned that someone get rid of those filthy pigs          scheming disrespectful boys.

# una lástima, le hace falta
# un hombre que sepa cuánto vale

*homenaje secreto a D.E.B.*

Está en la sala de operaciones y anestesiada puede oír que el equipo
de cirujanos especialmente reunido para estudiar su caso dice:
        nunca nunca hemos visto unas entrañas tan hermosas
unos labios tan expresivos
        un hígado tan sutilmente configurado
nunca nos ha tocado un aliento tan dulce
se nota que es buena cocinera
se nota que es un cuerpo hecho para el amor
y extasiados siguen abriendo y buscando
increíble ¿será posible que haya tenido hijos? ¿cómo si no hay rastros?
        ENAMORADOS
Ya les mostrará ya les dará su oportunidad cuando deban ayudarla a
bajarse de la cama en el camisón color lila y las chinelas de raso estilo
jean harlow.

# if only she had a guy to tell her how much she's worth

*secret homage to D.E.B.*

She is in the operating room and under anesthesia she can hear the
team of surgeons especially brought together to study her case say:
        never never have we seen such beautiful intestines
such expressive lips
        a liver so subtly configured
never has such a sweet breath touched us
you can see she is a good cook
you can see her body is made for love
and in ecstasy they keep opening and searching
incredible        is it possible that she may have had children? how
    if there are no signs?
        HEAD OVER HEELS
now she will show them now give them their chance when they have
to help her get out of the bed wearing the lilac-colored robe and the
ballet slippers jean harlow style.

THE AMERICAS

*Tent of Miracles*
Jorge Amado
Translated by Barbara Shelby Merello; new introduction by Ilan Stavans

*Tieta*
Jorge Amado
Translated by Barbara Shelby Merello; new introduction by Moacyr Scliar

*The Inhabited Woman*
Gioconda Belli
Translated by Kathleen March; new foreword by Margaret Randall

*Golpes bajos / Low Blows: Instantáneas / Snapshots*
Alicia Borinsky
Translated by Cola Franzen and the author; foreword by Michael Wood

*A World for Julius: A Novel*
Alfredo Bryce Echenique
Translated by Dick Gerdes; new foreword by Julio Ortega

*The Mexico City Reader*
Edited by Ruben Gallo

*Ballad of Another Time: A Novel*
José Luis González
Translated by Asa Zatz; introduction by Irene Vilar

*The Purple Land*
W. H. Hudson
New introduction by Ilan Stavans

*A Pan-American Life: Selected Poetry and Prose of Muna Lee*
Muna Lee
Edited and with biography by Jonathan Cohen;
foreword by Aurora Levins Morales

*The Bonjour Gene: A Novel*
J. A. Marzán
Introduction by David Huddle

*The Decapitated Chicken and Other Stories*
Horacio Quiroga
Selected and translated by Margaret Sayers Peden; introduction by Jean Franco

*San Juan: Ciudad Soñada*
Edgardo Rodríguez Juliá
Introduction by Antonio Skármeta

*San Juan: Memoir of a City*
Edgardo Rodríguez Juliá
Translated by Peter Grandbois; foreword by Antonio Skármeta

*The Centaur in the Garden*
Moacyr Scliar
Translated by Margaret A. Neves; new introduction by Ilan Stavans

*Preso sin nombre, celda sin número*
Jacobo Timerman
Forewords by Arthur Miller and Ariel Dorfman

*Prisoner without a Name, Cell without a Number*
Jacobo Timerman
Translated by Toby Talbot; new introduction by Ilan Stavans;
new foreword by Arthur Miller

*Life in the Damn Tropics: A Novel*
David Unger
Foreword by Gioconda Belli